"Justin, can't you just take me home?"

The sound of his name on Lila's lips touched him, and he felt himself shutting down, his barriers rising. He wouldn't allow himself any messy emotional attachments. He just had a job to do. "We're not dealing with ordinary criminals here. You don't want these people discovering who you are, where you live, where your family lives. If they followed us, you'd never be safe."

Lila breathed out, "I'm scared."

He stood rooted to the floor, fighting impulses he'd long held at bay. The sincerity of her emotions touched a core within him, a core he guarded and protected with a hardened shell. How had she insinuated herself there so easily?

He picked up his bags.

"We need to leave, Lila. You'll be safe with me."

CAROL ERICSON

THE STRANGER AND I

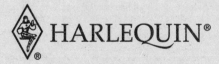

HARLEQUIN®

TORONTO • NEW YORK • LONDON
AMSTERDAM • PARIS • SYDNEY • HAMBURG
STOCKHOLM • ATHENS • TOKYO • MILAN • MADRID
PRAGUE • WARSAW • BUDAPEST • AUCKLAND

To my husband, Neil, and our two boys for their
enduring love and support. *Ustedes son mis héroes.*

ISBN-13: 978-0-373-69301-6
ISBN-10:   0-373-69301-X

THE STRANGER AND I

ABOUT THE AUTHOR

Carol Ericson lives with her husband and two sons in Southern California, home of state-of-the-art cosmetic surgery, wild freeway chases, palm trees bending in the Santa Ana winds and a million amazing stories. These stories, along with hordes of virile men and feisty women, clamor for release from Carol's head. It makes for some interesting headaches, until she sets them free to fulfill their destinies and her readers' fantasies. To find out more about Carol, her books and her strange headaches, please visit her Web site at www.carolericson.com, "where romance flirts with danger."

Books by Carol Ericson

HARLEQUIN INTRIGUE
1034—THE STRANGER AND I

CAST OF CHARACTERS

Lila Monroe—Her trusting nature lands her in the middle of a terrorist plot. Now she has to place her life and her heart in the hands of the one man who can save both.

Justin Vidal—He protects his damaged psyche with a stone barricade, but from the moment Lila Monroe shows up on his doorstep, she chips away at the fortress until he learns to live... and love again.

Chad Delaney—His cryptic last words send the terrorists and the people who track them down on a wild goose chase along the U.S.-Mexico border.

Prasad Mansour—An American Muslim, is he loyal to his country or the fanatical wing of his religion?

Victoria Lang—This sultry operative dies in the service of her country. Or does she?

Leo Caine—HIA field office supervisor juggles an explosive mix: top-secret clearance and a taste for the high life.

Danny Molina—Shunned in Mexico, betrayed in Costa Rica, he turns to the only man he can trust.

Tyler Stone—Lila's son, a math wiz who uses his skills to help save his mother, must now put aside his distrust and bond with the man who's destined to rescue her.

Chapter One

The sharp snap jarred Lila out of an uneasy sleep. She bolted upright. Shrugging off the coarse, itchy blanket, she peered through the dirty car window into the dark, now-silent night. Where'd Chad go?

She glanced into the front seat. The keys dangled from the ignition, and her purse rested on the passenger seat where she'd left it before crawling into the back for a nap. Her mouth dry, she inhaled the mist seeping through the open window in the front.

Pressing her nose against the cool glass, she tried to focus on the dark shapes etched in the muted moonlight. Rubbing her eyes, she rolled down the window, catching the salty air on her tongue. A grove of palmetto and conical boojum trees created a thick barrier halting the encroachment of the narrow gravel road.

She heard it again, a crack cutting through the air. That same sound had permeated her sleep, dredging her up to this muddled state of consciousness. Instinctively, she opened her mouth to call out to Chad, but prickles of uncertainty danced along the back of her neck. She snapped her lips shut.

Chad told her earlier that he had to make a stop to meet someone before they crossed the border, but in this deserted spot? Didn't make sense.

She grasped the car-door handle, easing it forward and nudging the door open with her knee. The dome light flickered and faded, failing to shed any light on her predicament.

"Damn," she muttered, "broken like everything else in this crappy car."

She placed a sandaled foot on a thick carpet of plant life that muffled her step.

And slid into the unknown.

Leaving the door open, she stole through the cluster of trees toward a new sound. Voices. Did Chad find his friend? The tone of the voices didn't sound very friendly. She crouched behind some underbrush that skirted a small clearing.

Angry words punctuated the night air. She strained to understand them, inching toward another bush to gain a clear view of the open space.

She gaped at the man kneeling on the ground with his hands secured behind his back. A streak of what looked like blood stained his right cheek. Chad. And those men didn't look like friends.

A thickset figure stood before Chad, holding a thin whip. Another, taller man pointed a gun at Chad's head. The man with the whip snapped it and barked out a question in a foreign language. Chad shook his head, earning him a swipe across his bare chest. A thin line of blood sprang up. He jerked his head back, his long blond hair swinging behind him.

Lila bit the inside of her cheek to keep from screaming. The metallic taste of her own blood spiked her tongue. She couldn't understand the stocky man. Her brow creased. The language he spoke didn't remotely resemble Spanish.

Chad's tormentors had their backs to her, so she poked her head above the shrubbery to get his attention.

His half-closed eyes widened for a moment. He shook his head and groaned out, "No," before dropping his chin to his chest.

Was that meant for her? She ducked.

Crouching, she scanned the ground for a heavy rock or a stick. She needed a weapon. She glanced back at the gun glinting in the moonlight and froze. A rock, no matter how heavy, couldn't take on a firearm.

Her eyes darted to the other side of the clearing. Should she create a disturbance? Could Chad escape? Eyeing his limp form, she doubted he could make much of an effort. No, she had to get away and find help if she hoped to save Chad.

From their language, she knew the men weren't Mexican Federales. At least Chad hadn't broken any Mexican laws to get into this predicament. Or had he? What did she really know about Chad Delaney beyond what his casual chatter revealed during the three carefree days they'd spent together?

The man with the whip growled out another question. Raising his head, Chad gasped out an answer in the same language.

Wrong answer.

The whip shot out again, this time catching Chad across his bare thigh. Lila twitched with the impact, the sting resonating on her own flesh.

Chad threw his head back and yelled, *"El túnel está aquí…"* The tall man fired his gun. Chad pitched face forward in the dirt.

Her stomach lurched. She ground her teeth together to subdue the sour lump of terror rising from her gut.

Her eyes burned into the backs of the men now standing over Chad's lifeless body, but her feet stayed as rooted to the ground as the thick brush that ringed the clearing.

Branches crackled and the trees across from her parted, ejecting two more men brandishing guns. As they cursed in Spanish, Lila peeled her feet from the ground and backed up one step at a time. The thick, springy undergrowth silenced her footsteps, but the two sets of men were too busy screaming at each other to hear anything anyway.

Once free of the bushes, she spun and ran for the car. Her heart ricocheted in her chest. The sound of her own terror roared in her ears like a wild beast. She tripped on a gnarled root. She sprawled forward, flinging her arms out in front of her. The sharp edges of the leaves and twigs covering the ground bit into her palms and knees. She dragged herself up. She plunged ahead, ignoring the pain that pierced her ankle.

Staccato blasts echoed in the clearing.

More tree branches snapped.

Were they chasing her?

A sob ripped through her throat. A scream penetrated the mist. She couldn't tell if it belonged to her or one of the four men involved in the shoot-out behind her.

She lunged at the car and gripped the door handle. As she yanked the door open, her breath raked through her lungs. She twisted her head over her shoulder to peer into the moon-smudged darkness.

No one followed. Were they all dead? She didn't plan to stick around for the autopsies.

Dropping onto the driver's seat, she grabbed at the keys in the ignition and cranked them forward. The engine sprang to life, and she ground the gearshift into Reverse. She stomped on the accelerator without even looking behind her. The back door of the car, which she'd left open, slammed shut. Her heart rate charged up another notch.

The tires crunched on the gravel, spewing dust and grit in their wake. Once she hit the paved road, Lila spun the steering wheel, threw the gear shift into first and gunned it. The car lurched and almost stalled before she shoved it into second and then third gear. Giving a protesting whine, the car straightened out on the asphalt and hurtled forward into the night. Her eyes picked out a Jeep pulled over to the side of the road. Stopping was not an option.

Lila clutched the steering wheel, her eyes darting back and forth between the road in front of her and the rearview mirror. Surely the men who murdered Chad heard her escape but still nobody came. And who were the other two, Chad's friends?

She careened off the main road onto a smaller one that paralleled the coast. Her mind buzzed with shock and fear as she continued driving on for another hour.

Peeling her eyes from their constant vigil between the road ahead and the one receding in her mirror, she glanced down at the instrument panel. She needed gas. She needed food. And she needed to harness her galloping thoughts.

Calling the police in Mexico spelled trouble. What if Chad planned to meet this friend for a drug deal or something? Would the police arrest her as his accomplice? A cold fear grabbed her gut.

The light broke to the east, filtering through the haze, working its fingers through the gaps in the brown hills. A battered sign announced the next town, Loma Vista.

She pulled up to a gas pump in front of a dusty roadside café on the outskirts of town. As she filled the tank, her hands shook and the gas sloshed from the nozzle dribbling down the side of the car.

Leaning into the window, she grabbed her purse and walked toward the little café to pay and get something to eat.

The man at the counter smiled, his teeth gleaming against his brown skin. "*Hola, señorita.* You pay for gas?"

Lila answered, "*Hola,* yes, the gas, and could I please have some huevos rancheros and a cup of coffee?"

The few patrons at the counter ignored her. Americans close to the border were commonplace, even off the main road.

When she pulled out her wallet, a white envelope, with her first name scribbled across the front, slid to the floor. Wrinkling her brow, she picked it up.

She paid the clerk and carried the envelope to a table by the window. She ripped it open and pulled out a single sheet of folded paper.

Lila, if you're reading this then something happened to me. If I don't return to the car, take it across the border and go straight to the name and address at the bottom of this page. Don't call the police or go to the Federales. I'm sorry to drag you into this, but when I saw you standing at the side of the road it was a stroke of luck for me. I'm afraid it was an ill omen for you, but once you deliver the car and tell Justin what happened you'll be fine. Again, I'm sorry…

The name *Justin Vidal* and an address appeared at the bottom of the page.

The proprietor put her plate of eggs on the table. She jumped.

He frowned. "*Lo siento, señorita.* I scare you?"

Shaking her head and covering the letter with her hand, she gave a hollow laugh. "Oh no, no. I'm just tired. That's why I need the coffee. *Gracias.*"

He shrugged, put the coffee cup on the table next to the plate and shuffled back to the counter.

Clutching her fork, she stared at the letter. Chad expected trouble and picked her up anyway. She jabbed at the eggs on her plate and speared a forkful into her mouth. As she chewed, she ground her teeth together.

He used her to make sure the news of his demise would get safely back to this Justin Vidal, whoever he was.

She swallowed and sighed, her anger evaporating as quickly as it collected. The man just died. She could at least try to honor his last wishes, unless there were drugs in the car. She wouldn't go down that road again.

She screwed her eyes shut, trying to block out the vision of Chad plunging forward into the dirt. Before the others arrived, Chad and the two men had been speaking a strange language. Arabic? She didn't see the men as clearly as Chad's battered body claimed all her attention. Why did a man like Chad, a surfer on vacation in Mexico, speak Arabic?

The other two came charging in speaking Spanish. Were they all connected, or did the Mexicans stumble onto the scene as she did? With guns? Chad had some strange friends.

Puffing her cheeks, she blew out a breath of air and swept her change off the table into her hand. While putting her change away in her wallet, she flipped it open to the plastic insert. With her fingertip, she traced the outline of a face in the photo. Tyler.

She finished her eggs and swallowed the rest of her coffee, grimacing at its bitter taste. Calling a farewell to the man at the counter, she walked out to the car. She glanced up and down the road.

Before proceeding any further with this wild scheme or getting in any deeper, she wanted to make sure Chad didn't have anything illegal stashed in his trunk, making her an unwitting accomplice. Once was believable, twice was criminal.

In keeping with the car's battered condition, the trunk lock was broken. She eased open the trunk, tilting her head sideways to glimpse inside. Drawing her brows together, she reached out to pluck at what looked like a pile of clothes.

Her fingers touched clammy human flesh. She gasped and drew back as the trunk light illuminated the curled-up body of a man. She clamped her fist to her mouth.

She slammed the lid down and stood trembling. Her hand gripped the keys in the broken lock. Was this the friend Chad went to meet? She craned her neck to glance into the café at the same bunch of men huddled over the counter. Nobody even looked out the window.

Could she dump the body out here? *Don't be ridiculous.* She'd never get away with that.

Should she tell someone inside the restaurant to call the Federales? Chad's letter specifically ordered her not to do that, but what did she owe Chad? He dragged her into this mess and then got himself murdered, but maybe he knew calling the Federales would get her into trouble now.

The screen door of the café banged open, and the proprietor stepped out onto the sagging porch. "Is everything okay, *señorita?* Your car okay?"

She yelled back, "*Está bien.* It's okay."

He stood outside watching her, and she made one of her hasty decisions. *Oh hell, I'm going to do what Chad asked me to do in that letter. Dead body or no dead body.*

She waved to the man on the porch and slid into the car.

Taking it slow and easy, she got back on the main road toward Tijuana and the border. She joined the line of cars crawling through the border stop. She licked her dry lips and called over one of the many vendors threading their way through the cars. After a few minutes of haggling, she bought a large, gaudy sombrero and a donkey puppet on strings in an attempt to appear like a normal tourist, even though she felt far from normal. Tyler would like the puppet anyway.

As she inched the dirty little car forward, her mouth got drier and drier. Her hands gripped the steering wheel until her knuckles bleached white. She drew a ragged breath and grabbed the water bottle lying on the seat next to her. She grimaced at the film of sediment at the bottom of the bottle and wet her lips with the warm, stale water.

Releasing the steering wheel, she flexed her fingers and coached herself. "You can do this, Lila."

The Border Patrol agent approached her car, and she turned down the radio and rolled down the window. His dark sunglasses hid his eyes, reflecting her face. Her lips peeled back in a smile.

He ducked his head. "Good morning, ma'am. What was the reason for your visit to Mexico?"

"Just came over as a tourist." She didn't want to get into any long explanations with him about her research as a marine biologist.

Gesturing to the car, he said, "Looks like you've been driving quite a bit."

She shrugged. "Just down the coast and back." Sucking in a breath, she held her smile and waited.

He shook his head. "It's not a great idea for a woman to drive alone in Mexico."

Stepping back, he waved her through. "Have a nice day."

She expelled her breath, and breezed across the border into the United States of America.

Once she reached the border town of Nestor, she pulled off the road into the parking lot of a shopping center. She grabbed the grubby street map shoved in the door's side pocket. After jotting down the directions to the address in Chad's note, she took off to deliver the bad news and the dead body to Justin Vidal.

Cruising into San Diego, she searched for the address among streets that twisted and turned through hills and canyons. She found it tucked away on a quiet block dense with trees. A high fence and lush vegetation obscured the house from the road.

She pulled up across the street and, still favoring her sore ankle, walked through the gate up to a large wooden deck.

She rang the doorbell and knotted her hands in front of her. What was she doing? She had a dead guy in her trunk. She should just call the police right now. She spun on her heel, when a gruff voice from behind the door stopped her.

"Who is it?"

She gulped. "Ah, you don't know me, but I met Chad Delaney in Mexico, and he gave me a lift, and—"

The thick wooden door jerked open. A strong arm shot out and dragged her across the threshold. That same arm encircled her neck, pinning her back against a body as hard as granite.

She clawed at his arm and stomped down on his foot in a futile struggle. A click close to her ear made her freeze. Out of the corner of her eye, she saw the barrel of a very big gun.

The low voice, as smooth as silky, dark chocolate but not as sweet, purred in her ear. "That's better. Now, who the hell are you, and where's Chad?"

A river of anger coursed through her veins, washing away the fear. She did everything Chad asked of her, and his so-called friend planned to repay her with a bullet in the head?

She gasped out, "If you'd get your arm off my neck, I could tell you."

The man grunted and released her so quickly, she stumbled. She pivoted and looked up into a pair of tawny-colored eyes glinting with sparks of anger. The man's intense stare plucked an answering chord in her chest, and she raised her hand to cover her heart. Then her gaze fell to the gun still aimed in her direction.

"And stop pointing that thing at me. I've had just about enough of you and Chad, and, and…" She sagged against the door while hot tears scalded her cheeks. She sensed movement from the stranger, but he made no attempt to comfort her.

Comfort? Yeah, like a rattlesnake.

Damn, she hated crying. It never solved anything. Didn't do much good when her father died, and wouldn't do much good now in the face of this man's smoldering fierceness.

Dragging a hand across her face, she heaved herself off the door. She glanced up through wet lashes at the imposing figure still standing in front of her, sinewy arms crossed over an unyielding chest. He watched her through narrowed eyes.

Tiger's eyes.

But at least the gun had disappeared.

She rubbed her nose with the back of her hand and croaked, "Can I sit down?"

He stepped back and nodded toward a chair by the window, his dark, wet hair falling over one eye. She limped to the hard chair and perched on the edge.

"Who are you, and where's Chad?"

Gripping her knees, she drew a shaky breath. "Chad's dead."

The man in front of her swore softly but didn't move, except for a twitching muscle in his jaw. Some emotion flickered in his eyes. Fear? Regret?

He intoned, "Go on."

She dragged her hands through her tangled hair as she continued. "I met Chad three days ago just outside of Playa Roja. I'm a marine biologist, a graduate student at U.C. San Diego, and I went to Mexico to conduct a study of the marine life off the coast there."

His lean jaw relaxed a little, and encouraged, she plunged ahead. "My car broke down, and Chad came by and gave me a lift."

The man's breath hissed out between his clenched teeth, but he said nothing. Every taut muscle in his body signaled danger.

She faltered. "I—I… He said he was driving back up across the border and could take me all the way into San Diego. We planned to drive all night, crossing the border in the early morning, but last night Chad mentioned he had to make a quick stop to meet a friend."

Interrupting her for the first time since her monologue began, he asked, "Did he tell you why? Did he tell you his business in Mexico?"

She shook her head. "He didn't say why he was meeting the friend, but he told me he came to Mexico for the surfing."

Sinking into the chair across from her, he extended his long legs in front of him, crossing his ankles. "How'd he die?"

Lila shot him a look from under her eyelashes. His expressiveness rivaled the Terminator's. Looked about as hard, too. "I climbed into the back seat to get some sleep, and when I woke up Chad was gone. He'd parked down a gravel access road at the edge of a

clump of trees. I had a strange feeling when I woke up, so I crept to the clearing and saw Chad with his hands behind
him and two men questioning him. One had a gun and one had a whip or something. They asked him a question in a foreign language, he answered in the same language, and the one with the gun shot him."

The man sprang forward, his eyes wide. "You mean, you witnessed Chad's murder? Did these people see you?"

Was that concern for her? Encouraged by this first sign of emotion other than anger, she answered, "Yeah, I saw everything, but they didn't see me. I hid behind some bushes." She tilted her head. "I think Chad saw me though."

He waited in silence, his muscles perfectly still, but even in repose the man buzzed with activity, a thinly contained restlessness.

Slumping in her chair, she massaged her temples. "After the men killed Chad, two other men came crashing through the bushes, yelling and screaming in Spanish."

His brows shot up. "Two more men? What happened after that?"

She hunched her shoulders. "I didn't want to stick around to find out. While I ran back to the car, I heard gunfire and a babble of voices. I got to the car and took off." She bit her lip. "They probably heard me drive away, but I don't think they followed me. Too busy shooting at each other."

He shifted in the chair and ground out, "You don't think they followed you? That's rich. You probably led them right to my doorstep."

He jumped up and peered between the plain white blinds as if expecting to see the two men standing on his deck.

With his back to her, Lila now saw the gun shoved in the waistband of his faded jeans. His damp T-shirt clung to his back, outlining his muscles. Must've just gotten out of the shower.

He spoke over his shoulder, "What are you doing here anyway, and why didn't you call the Federales? Come to think of it, why didn't you call the U.S. authorities once you crossed the border?"

She took a deep shuddering breath. "Chad left me a note."

Fumbling in her purse, she withdrew the slip of paper and handed it to him.

He opened it and scanned the contents.

"Chad asked me not to go to the Federales, told me to come straight to you." She added, "Y-you are Justin Vidal, aren't you?"

He snorted. "Little late to be asking that question, isn't it? Yeah, I'm Vidal. This still doesn't explain why you didn't call the police when you got across the border. You took a big chance coming here. For all you know, Chad and I could be drug dealers."

Wrinkling her nose, she said, "Yeah, I thought of that, but Chad didn't strike me as the drug-dealer type. And, well, I liked him. I wanted to carry out his last wishes. They *were* his last wishes."

Her nose stung with tears, and she rubbed it. She did not want to cry in front of this man again. Useless to cry anyway. He seemed immune to her feelings, immune to all feelings, including his own.

He glanced up from the letter, his eyes traveling over her body, as if seeing her for the first time. His gaze left pinpricks of excitement in its wake. Great, she had an insane attraction to a robot.

His lips tightened into a grim smile. "I see."

Lila folded her arms across her chest. She wasn't sure what he saw, hopefully it didn't include her peaked nipples, but she had more of her story to tell. "There's something else."

Waving the letter at her, he said, "Go on."

She cleared her throat. "There's a dead body in the trunk of Chad's car. I think it might be that friend he planned to meet."

The letter fluttered to the floor, as Justin Vidal took a step back, one eyebrow lifted in patent disbelief. He whispered, "What?"

Feeling more than a little satisfied that she'd elicited some solid emotion from the man, she enunciated, "A dead body."

He growled, "I heard you the first time. I can't believe you drove across the border with a dead body in the trunk of your car."

She corrected, "Chad's car."

His hand sliced through the air, and she ducked.

"Whatever. What's it doing there?"

She launched into an explanation of how she'd stopped for gas, checked the trunk to make sure Chad wasn't concealing anything illegal and discovered the body of a man curled up inside the trunk.

She stood up as she finished. "You see, that's another reason why I didn't want to call the authorities. I didn't want to come under any suspicion."

"And your actions up to now haven't been suspicious in the least."

She shook her head. "I thought you'd be happy I came straight to you."

She expected a better reception from Justin Vidal than this. She'd just been through hell, and he was treating her like the enemy.

Planting herself in front of him, she wedged her hands on her hips. "I want some answers now. Who are you anyway and who's Chad and what was he really doing in Mexico?"

"That—" he gripped her arm "—is not important right now. All you have to know is that we're the good guys. Let's go see this dead body, if he's really dead."

His touch seared her skin. How could such a cold man cause a wave of heat to rush through her body? "Yeah, you're the good guys. Chad brought me into this mess, and you've done nothing but manhandle me since I got here." She shook off his hand before his scorching touch caused her to melt in a puddle at his feet. "Will you please get off me?"

Those tawny eyes darkened as he dropped her arm. He limped to the front door and, hanging back, gestured her through first.

What was he worried about? He had the gun.

She glanced down at his bare feet. "Why are you limping?"

His lips twisted. "You stomped on my foot."

Was that supposed to be a smile?

"Sorry." As she brushed by him out the front door, he recoiled. She rolled her eyes. Man, did he have issues.

They hobbled into the street, empty except for a few cars parked along the side. She led him to Chad's battered little car and flipped up the trunk. Her mouth fell open as first she stared into the trunk and then turned to Justin Vidal, studying her through narrowed eyes.

Frantically, she plunged into the trunk, clawing at her bags, her diving gear and a tire iron, to no avail.

The dead man was gone.

Chapter Two

"He's gone." The woman's arms flailed in the air as she looked up and down the street, as if expecting her "dead man" to suddenly materialize.

Justin crossed his arms and watched her dive into the trunk again. Chad must've been out of his mind picking up this woman. Chad was dead. His throat tightened. Why'd the impulsive fool go it alone? And why did Molina choose that moment to go to Costa Rica?

Chad must've discovered something after he placed that call from Mexico City, but the note held no clues unless Chad left him something in the car. Did the woman know more than she'd revealed? Who were the Mexicans who came onto the scene? Were they working with Chad? Chad's killers would've pursued her and killed her—unless they died at the scene themselves.

Trust Chad to involve a woman. He probably slept with her. Chad could just about get any woman to do anything for him after he took her to bed. In their line of work that talent definitely had its uses.

Justin eyed her slender form half buried in the trunk as

she clawed through its contents, probably searching for the dead man. Chad always did have good taste in women.

Her head popped up, a tangled mass of blond curls framing her flushed face. "He was in here. I swear."

He said, "Maybe he wasn't dead. Maybe he just walked away. Did you see any wounds on the body, any blood? You check his pulse?"

Her deep blue eyes mirrored her confusion. "No, I didn't want to touch him."

He shot back, "Then how'd you know he was dead?"

She raked her hand through her hair. "I—I… He was in the trunk," she finished lamely.

"So?" The woman had about as much sense as a kitten in the rain. He squelched an urge to brush a lock of hair from her eye. The sooner he sent her on her way, the better.

Glancing back down at the gaping trunk now disgorging its contents, she asked, "Why would he be in the trunk otherwise?"

He surveyed the fins, oxygen tank and mask spilling out of the car. Chad didn't dive. "A man in the trunk of a car close to the U.S.–Mexican border isn't all that unusual. Maybe he climbed into the trunk when you stopped for food."

Her brow cleared as she nodded. "I get it. You and Chad aren't drug smugglers, you're people smugglers."

"We are not," he snapped. Actually, he had a sinking suspicion that the man in the trunk was Chad's informant. If so, they walked right into a trap. Did the informant somehow escape from the trunk? He had to find him, get information from him.

She smoothed her hands over her face and emerged

with a frown tugging at the corners of her full lips. Ever since she'd intruded on his space, her emotions had been galloping across her face in an everchanging kaleidoscope. An unwelcome stab of guilt pricked Justin's conscience, and an even more unwelcome jolt of desire knotted his gut.

"The less you know about us, the safer it is for you. I'll help you collect your things from Chad's car and give you a lift home. Your role in this little drama is over."

He examined the trunk's broken lock, which showed signs of tampering. Did the informant escape or did someone follow the woman here and remove him from the trunk? Icy fingers tripped up his spine.

"There's a trace of blood in here." As he ran his hands over the inside of the trunk, he heard the rumble of an engine build, its low roar coming closer until tires screeched around the corner. His head shot up. A dark sedan rocketed down the street toward them.

He yelled, "Get down."

Dragging a bag out of the trunk, she looked up, mouth agape. He tackled her. The car slowed down. He stuffed her under Chad's car with one hand, reaching for his Glock with the other. A bullet pierced the air, slamming into the curb beside him. He leveled his weapon at the hooded figure leaning out the car window and shot back.

Another bullet whizzed past his ear and clanged against the bumper. The soft body beneath him jerked. He fired once more at the retreating car before it sped around the corner, choking the air with exhaust.

The woman raised her head, her eyes occupying half her face. "Who was that? What's going on?"

He pulled her up. "Looks like you were followed after all or picked up at the border. Or that's your dead man taking revenge for his mode of transportation. You okay?"

Before she could answer, a man stepped out on his porch and yelled, "What the hell is going on out here?"

Justin waved his arm. "Just some kids lighting some leftover firecrackers. I chased them off."

"Damn kids." The man retreated, banging his screen door behind him.

Still clutching his gun at his side, Justin propelled the woman across the street and into his house. He yanked a duffel bag out of the closet and started shoveling clothes into it.

He said over his shoulder, "We have to get out of here." Turning, he saw her standing in the middle of the room knotting her hands in front of her.

He had no intention of becoming this woman's white knight, but he could show her a little courtesy for her trouble. He stopped packing. "Sit down. I'll get you a soda or something."

She shot a glance at the window, her breath coming in short spurts. "Will they come back?"

"Not now. They'll be afraid the gunshots will attract the police, but they won't stay away for long." He handed her a can of soda, and she gulped it. He studied her face, its delicate planes creased with anxiety. Damn Chad.

She lifted her eyes to his and the trust shining from them chipped at a hard corner of his heart. "Where are we going?" she asked.

"To safety. Is there anyone expecting you, family, husband?" He held his breath.

Her long, golden lashes swept down to veil her eyes

for a moment. "No, I'm not expected back from Mexico for another week." A grin twisted her lips. "I left early to get a jump on recording my research."

He returned the grin then finished packing. After dropping his bag by the door, he disconnected his laptop and stowed it in its case. He gave the small house a final glance. He'd have to abandon it, just as he had a few others along the way.

His gaze shifted to the woman on his couch, her feet curled beneath her long tanned legs. She held the can of soda pressed against her cheek, her eyes closed. He realized with a start he didn't even know her name. How did Chad address her in the letter? Lisa? Lily?

They had a long drive ahead of them, and he had to call her something. "What's your name?"

She drained the can of soda and answered, "Lila Monroe." She hesitated. "Justin, why do I have to come with you? Why can't you just take me home?"

The sound of his name on her lips touched him, and he felt his face shutting down, his barriers rising. He wouldn't allow himself any messy emotional attachments. He just had a job to do. "We're not dealing with ordinary criminals here. You don't want these people discovering who you are, where you live, where your family lives. If I dropped you off at your home now and they followed us, you'd never be safe."

She breathed out, "I'm scared."

He stood rooted to the floor, fighting impulses he'd long held at bay. The sincerity of her emotions touched a core within him, a core he guarded and protected with a hardened shell. How had she insinuated herself there so easily?

He picked up his bags. "We need to leave, Lila. You'll be safe where I'm taking you. Get another soda for the road, and grab one for me, too. We'll get something to eat along the way."

Stowing his bags in the bed of his truck along with the camping gear he always kept there, he ordered Lila to climb in the cab and wait. He stole out to Chad's car, keeping his weapon ready, and grabbed the gear from the open trunk. He swept the contents of the glove compartment into a bag and then loaded everything into his truck.

Lila sat in the passenger seat staring ahead at nothing, her face pale beneath sun-kissed skin. Justin cursed Chad and his lust, not for the first time. It was, however, the last. His breath hitched in his throat.

Starting the engine, he looked at his silent companion. "You ready?"

She closed her eyes and nodded. He expelled a breath, relaxing the muscles of his face. The eyes were supposed to be windows to the soul, and she seemed to peer right into his. The clear blue light from her eyes probed his inner depths, peeling back one layer of his defenses at a time. From the moment she appeared on his doorstep, he felt transparent under her gaze. And worse, she seemed to understand his defects and pity him for them.

Did she realize Chad's death lay at his door? Justin should've been a better mentor, should've been more forceful in telling Chad to hold tight until he got down there. He failed Chad just when Chad needed him most. That thought burned behind his eyes until he doused it. Better not go down that road.

After an hour's sleep, Lila stirred. Those impossible

golden curls shielded one half of her face. Her long lashes with their dark tips lay like a curve of velvet on her cheek. Her lips, even in repose, turned up at the corners.

A Pollyanna, that fit her perfectly, trusting, gullible. Fortunately this experience would cure her of that fatal flaw. Better to be on your guard.

She shoved her hair back from her face, blinking rapidly. Looking out the window, she asked, "Where are we?"

He answered, "Heading north on the I-15."

Turning her head toward him, she said, "The desert?"

"That's right. Do you mind driving for a while? I need to make a phone call and sort through Chad's stuff."

"I can drive, but can we pull over at a rest stop or something? I feel like I've just run a marathon, barefoot, and with wild beasts in pursuit."

His eyes roamed over her lithe body, and his hands itched to follow. He shook his head and laughed. "Looks like one of those wild beasts caught up with you."

She cocked her head at him. "You have a nice laugh. You should use it more often."

He gripped the steering wheel. "Not much to laugh at these days."

"You're wrong. The world holds a lot of laughter."

Not his world. He cut off her homily. "There's a rest area two miles ahead."

He maneuvered the car off the interstate and pulled in to the parking lot. While Lila slung a small bag over her shoulder and headed for the restrooms, he leaned against the truck facing the highway.

The flat desert landscape offered safety. An occasional Joshua tree reached up to the sky, proclaiming its indomitability against the suffocating desert heat, but most of the plant life crouched in the hot sand, allowing the naked eye to see for miles.

A couple of truckers hogged several parking spaces between them, and a family with three kids ducked in and out of a large cooler, pulling out sandwiches and drinks. Justin's chest contracted as the father swung the youngest boy up on his shoulders for a trip to the vending machines.

Lila emerged from the restroom, her dusty denim shorts and wrinkled T-shirt replaced by a pair of khaki hiking shorts and a blue tank top, which exposed her toned arms. A tortoiseshell headband swept her hair off her face, although a few of those riotous curls found freedom. As she stood in front of him, he suppressed an urge to capture one of those ringlets and wrap it around his finger.

She held out her hand. "Keys?" He dropped them into her palm and tossed her bag in the back of the truck. He brought his laptop and the bag containing the contents of Chad's glove compartment into the front.

Adjusting the seat and starting the engine, she asked, "Same direction for a while?"

He nodded and flipped open his cell phone. Someone picked up after two rings.

He recited, "This is Lone Wolf 58634." Those searching blue eyes skimmed his profile, so he turned to look out the window at the lunarlike landscape.

The voice on the other end responded, "Hi, Justin,

this is Prasad. I mean, Warrior Sheikh 28221. What's the word, my man? When are you going to Mexico?"

Justin took a deep breath. "Sooner than I planned. Chad's dead."

Prasad choked out, "How'd it happen?"

"They shot him. Thank God they didn't do worse. I think he might've discovered something. Can't think why else he'd plow ahead like that without me."

"Where was Molina?"

"Following a lead in Costa Rica."

Justin could hear Prasad measuring his words. "Nobody's going to blame you. We all know how impulsive he is…was. How'd you find out? We haven't heard a word here."

Justin slid his eyes over to Lila, concentrating on the road in front of her. She didn't fool him. She'd been soaking up every word. "He picked up a woman. She witnessed the murder, then hightailed it out of there."

Prasad gasped and then chuckled. "Figures there'd be a woman in the mix. Is she hot?"

Justin avoided taking inventory of the lovely lady in the driver's seat and grunted, "Yeah." He turned up the air-conditioning.

Prasad continued, "How'd she find you?"

"Chad left her a note with my name and address."

Prasad exclaimed, "And she actually came straight to you instead of the Federales? Wow, Chad must've really done a number on her. You gotta admire the guy. I'm glad he went out in a blaze of glory. We should all be so lucky."

Shifting in his seat, Justin redirected the conversation, telling Prasad the rest of the story about the two

Mexicans who arrived on the scene, the missing body in the trunk and the shoot-out in the street.

Prasad whistled. "You've had a busy morning, and all I've been doing is monitoring a couple of databases. What do you think happened to the guy in the trunk?"

"Not sure. I think he may have been Chad's informant. They probably met and got ambushed. If he walked away from that trunk, I have to track him down."

"Yeah, good luck with that. Do you think the Mexicans who showed up on the scene were working with Chad? Did they kill his murderers?"

"Probably and maybe. The witness claims she wasn't followed, which only makes sense if the killers are dead."

"Then how'd their associates find your place?"

"They made Chad's car and picked it up at the border. She's lucky…" Lila aimed a sharp glance at him and he trailed off.

Prasad asked, "You discover yet what Chad was in such a fever pitch to find down there that it got him killed? Anything to do with this chatter we're hearing about a terrorist attack on our soil?"

"I don't know, but I have a computer disk from his car, and I'm going to pop it in my laptop once I get off the phone. One more thing, Prasad, I'm coming in, and I'm bringing the woman with me. I didn't want to risk taking her home when we might be followed, but you guys can safely drop her back in. They don't know who she is."

Prasad assured him they'd be there for the rest of the night and could resettle the witness.

Justin set up his laptop and inserted the disk, ignoring Lila's penetrating gaze.

She said, "Are you going to tell me who you are now…Lone Wolf?"

He stopped tapping the keyboard. She had a point. She'd been on the express train to hell and back and deserved to know. "You've heard of the Department of Homeland Security?"

She waved her tapered fingers. "Of course, the department that brought us color-coded threat levels."

"Right. We're a covert offshoot of that department called Homeland Intelligence Agency or 'hiya' as we fondly call ourselves."

Those lovely lips tightened into a smirk. "As in, 'Hiya, we're just a bunch of friendly guys and gals'?"

He threw his head back and laughed. "Yeah, something like that. We're your best friend if you can give us information about terrorists slipping across our borders."

Her mouth formed a perfect O, which was way too kissable for comfort. "You're kidding. That's what Chad was doing in Mexico?"

"Working undercover…disguised as a surfer. Good disguise, huh?"

Her eyes shimmered with unshed tears as she turned to him. "Yeah, that long blond hair, tanned body, devil-may-care attitude. Perfect disguise."

Her voice broke, and his gut clenched. Oh, yeah, Chad really did a number on her. Justin left her alone with her grief.

After a few moments and a few sniffles, she tilted her chin toward the laptop. "You find anything yet?"

He'd been scanning the files on the disk, but they contained old news. "No, nothing we hadn't already gone through together. He called me from Mexico City. Must've been a few days before he picked you up. We've been searching for a tunnel from Mexico to the U.S., and he made contact with some coyotes down there."

Her brow creased, and he continued. "The guys who help illegals cross the border. But the illegals we're after aren't the ones scrambling to get here to find work. We're looking for the ones intent on exploding bombs in our shopping malls or on trains or buses."

She squinted at the asphalt in front of her, chewing her lip. A tunnel? A memory she'd been trying to suppress began solidifying in her mind. Chad kneeling in the dirt. The brutal whip slicing his body. The blood. His long hair swinging back. The gunshot. And before the gunshot? *El túnel está aquí.*

She jerked the steering wheel, and Justin clutched at the computer. "Hey, watch the road. The highway still kills more people than terrorists do."

She whispered, "*El túnel.*"

His eyes glinted as they bored into her. "What did you say?"

She repeated, "*Túnel, el túnel está aquí.* That's why he spoke in Spanish. They didn't understand Spanish. He shouted that to me."

Justin snapped the laptop shut and turned to her. "Are you telling me Chad yelled out 'The tunnel is here' before those men executed him?"

Bobbing her head up and down, she exclaimed, "That's exactly what I mean. He found this tunnel you're looking for. It must've been right there where they killed him. Maybe he didn't know that when he wrote me the note. He discovered it, or his contact told him, and they surprised them and killed them."

His tiger eyes formed two slits as he watched her. Now what? Was he going to get mad at her again? Just when he started to thaw out. He actually laughed… twice.

He spit out, "Why didn't you tell me this before?"

She tossed her hair. "You're unbelievable. I just solved your case for you, and you're mad because I didn't do it sooner."

He inclined his head and compressed his lips before stating, "You haven't solved the case, and this is no TV cop show."

Scowling at him, she said, "I didn't remember what he said because I've been trying to forget what I saw and heard in that clearing."

The deep lines at the sides of his mouth retreated. "I'm sorry. Thanks for telling me what you remembered, and you're probably right. He discovered the tunnel, and they discovered him."

She felt a warm glow. That's more like it. She tapped her fingers on the steering wheel. "How do you think that guy got in the trunk?"

He shrugged his broad shoulders. "The terrorists ambushed them and killed him first before you woke up. What I don't understand is how they stashed the body in the trunk without waking you up or seeing you."

She snapped her fingers. "Chad covered me with a blanket. The night was pretty warm and I didn't remember having a blanket, but when I woke up I was completely covered. Maybe Chad hid me on purpose."

Clapping her hand over her mouth, she uttered, "Oh my God, what if they had found me in that car?"

He touched her shoulder. A current sizzled from his fingertips to her bare skin. She searched his face to see if he felt it, too.

His amber eyes flickered, and then he drew back. "You must lead a charmed life. Could you find that spot again?"

"Are you letting me in?"

He pressed his back against the truck's door. "Letting you in?"

The man had more nerve endings than an exposed tooth. She held up one hand. "I mean, are you allowing me to help?"

He relaxed. "If you can get me as close as possible to that spot, that'd be a big help."

"I think I can do that." She mentally converted the hours she drove into miles, and remembered the little town where she stopped for food and gas. Yeah, she could give him that.

Then maybe they could get her home, and she could call Mom and Tyler. She'd leave them out of this until the HIA could get her safely back to her apartment in San Diego. Then this strange, bottled-up man could get back to his job alone, and she could get back to her life.

She'd have to start pulling back on the strings that attached her to him. He was a wounded bird if she ever saw one, as damaged as any sea creature she helped to restore to its habitat. He had his own habitat, that sterile house where he took tea with anger and fear. He couldn't even express sadness at the death of his colleague, even though she could read the pain haunting his eyes. Was he afraid if he let go he'd never find his way back to that barren shore he called a life?

Some people were past saving, better to concentrate on the ones who still had hope. She heard Gareth's mocking voice whisper, "Sap." Where he was concerned, she'd been a sap. And in that incident with Adam. She shuddered.

She hadn't been wrong about Chad, though. In the end, she couldn't save him, but she'd helped him. Shifting her eyes to the silent man next to her intent on the computer screen, she wondered if she was wrong about him. To save him would be a challenge beyond even her abilities.

They'd been on the road for nearly three hours. The moist ocean breezes of San Diego had long since been replaced by arid gusts that needled their flesh. Justin told her to pull over so he could take over driving duty once more. Before changing places, they stretched their legs outside the truck.

The shimmering heat rose like seaweed from the desert floor. Justin, hands on hips, drilled the horizon with his piercing gaze. He carried himself with the loose-limbed grace of an athlete. He'd deceived her with his strength when he'd yanked her into his house, impressing her as a huge, powerful figure. He had power all right and stood over six feet tall. But even though his body was taut, he was no bulging muscleman.

As if sensing her scrutiny, he turned and grinned. "You ready for the last leg of the trip?" His smile banished all the pain and disillusionment from his face. What put it there?

"Yeah, I'm ready to say 'hiya' to hiya."

He shook his head as he climbed back into the truck. "This heat's getting to you."

Their last stop had been in Twentynine Palms where they fueled up and downed a couple of sports drinks along with some sandwiches. Justin promised her a shower and some rest at the HIA facility. She needed both.

They hurtled over the blazing asphalt of Highway 62, leaving Twentynine Palms and civilization in the dust. Justin turned down a road heading south. A gated structure, the color of the encroaching sand, took shape in the glimmering heat.

Lila quipped, "Will you have to kill me after I see the secret compound?"

A shadow passed over his face. "Don't joke about it."

They inched up to the gate, and he inserted a key card into a slot. The gate rolled back on squeaking wheels. He parked the truck and stepped out onto concrete, glittering with particles of sand. The facility looked deserted, but most of the agents parked their cars in the back.

His jaw tightened, and a pulse throbbed in his throat. All his senses danced on the head of a pin. He sniffed the air, his nostrils flaring at the faint, acrid odor of gunpowder. Range practice?

Lila chirped, "Is it always so quiet here?"

He felt for the gun he'd just shoved into his gun bag along with his backup and ascended the steps to the entrance. He punched the intercom. No answer. Swiping his sweaty hand across his T-shirt, he flipped open the print reader with his other hand. He pressed his thumb against the reader and said, "Lone Wolf 58634."

The lock on the gunmetal-gray door clicked. He

withdrew a badge and flashed it at the reader. A second click. Shoving the door open, he stepped over the threshold. The familiar whirring and buzzing noises filtered out from the data lab in the back.

Victoria Lang sauntered into the hallway holding a pink-frosted cupcake, an overnight bag slung over one shoulder. "Oh, it's you. Prasad said you were coming in. Guess we didn't hear the intercom."

Justin expelled a breath and eyed the cupcake. Lifting one eyebrow, he asked, "One of your creations?"

Victoria scooped at the icing with a long, manicured fingernail and licked it. "Yeah, it's Dave's birthday. There's more in the back."

He gestured to her bag. "Are you off?"

She lifted the shoulder with the bag. "I'm leaving tomorrow morning, taking R & R in Vegas for a few days. Is this the witness?"

Before he could answer, she extended a sticky hand to Lila. "I'm Victoria Lang. Glad you came forward."

Justin made a terse introduction. "This is Lila." Victoria didn't need to know Lila's last name. Nobody did.

Lila said, "I don't think I had a choice."

Victoria shook her head so that her sleek black hair rippled over her shoulders. "We all have choices. Looks like Chad made a dumb one."

Justin clenched his teeth. Was she blaming him for Chad's failure? She couldn't blame him any more than he blamed himself. "He was on the scent."

Waving her cupcake in the air, Victoria said, "Yeah, yeah, but you'd never put anyone else in danger, Justin, except maybe yourself."

He asked, "Anyone hear from Molina yet?"

She lifted her dark sculpted brows. "Nope. You think he'd know about Chad's death. They were partners down there, albeit reluctant ones."

Prasad joined them in the hallway, his face drawn and too gaunt for a man his age.

Justin nodded to the younger man. "You okay?"

Prasad shrugged thin shoulders that masked a tensile strength. "I can't say I'm surprised. Chad always did take more risks than anyone else."

The "except you" hung in the air.

Justin brushed it away with the sweep of his arm. "You learn from his mistakes and go on, but it can happen to any one of us, even you, Warrior Sheikh."

Victoria snorted. "You still using that code name, Prasad? Dream on."

He countered, "Yeah, okay, Amazon Goddess."

"Wow, would you be S.O.L. if you were out in the field and needed assistance from me? I'll have you know, I'm now Lady Hawk."

Dropping a curve of long dark lashes over one eye, she winked at Lila and said, "Our boss has an exaggerated flair for the dramatic."

Justin grumbled, "Or the ridiculous." He gestured toward Lila, "Prasad, this is Lila, the witness I told you about."

Lila's cheeks grew pink under Prasad's scrutiny, and Justin stepped between them. Prasad didn't need to know any details, either. Justin asked, "Is Leo in?"

Victoria answered, "No, he hasn't been around much. Phones in from San Diego, gives us orders. You know Leo."

Justin knew his boss hankered after a promotion. More office work. More money. Less danger. Hell, the man had a family, two teenagers ready to start college soon. He deserved a breather.

Prasad said, "I called him about Chad. The news hit him hard."

"Leo always has his favorites." Victoria directed a pointed glance at Justin.

He turned his back on her. Leo had been his mentor in the early days, but Justin didn't need him now. Just complicated things, like Justin's own mentoring relationship with Chad and Prasad complicated things. His own father had failed as a role model, so what business did he have trying to guide others?

They all walked together into the data lab where three agents tapped away at keyboards in front of computer screens with one hand, balancing cupcakes in the other. They looked up at Justin's entrance and crowded around him to glean the details of Chad's murder.

He revealed only the basics as he intercepted Lila's puzzled look and finished, "Lila's going to show me the site of Chad's execution on the interactive map in the back and I'll go down to Mexico in the next few days to check it out."

Dave, the birthday boy, asked, "So you think they followed her?"

Justin replied, "Haven't figured that out yet, but if the Mexicans killed the two dirtbags who murdered Chad, their accomplices probably waited for Chad's car at the border." He felt Lila tense by his side and all his nerve endings tingled with a desire to touch her, smooth away the worry lines between her eyebrows.

He steepled his fingers and shot her a look from beneath his eyelids. "She needs to get home safely. Maybe a helicopter ride into Lindbergh Field." *She'll be safe and I'll be safe.* The thought nibbled at the edges of his mind. Ridiculous.

Dave shoved his glasses back up his nose and pressed, "Are we debriefing her here? Did Chad say anything before he died?"

Justin quelled the agent's curiosity with a cold glance from narrowed eyes. "I already did that. Chad said nothing."

Dave stepped back, holding up his hands. "All right. Enough said."

Before Justin took Lila to the navigation room, Prasad announced, "I'm going into Twentynine Palms for rations to get us through the rest of the night. Anyone need anything?"

Dave protested, "Hey, it's not your turn. It's my turn to go in. You just want to see Janet."

Victoria explained, "Prasad met a cute Japanese woman who works at the shopping center in Twentynine Palms. A Muslim who practices Islam and a Buddhist. We keep telling him it's doomed."

Prasad laughed. "Lust conquers all."

He began taking orders for beef jerky, microwave popcorn and lattes while Justin and Lila retreated to the back room. A long night loomed ahead of them all.

As he punched the code in for the door, Lila asked, "Is that it? Just the six of you?"

"It varies, depending who's out in the field. The team's bigger but some of the agents are on assignment.

Danny Molina and I are stationed in Mexico right now. Chad was, too."

"Why weren't you down there with him?"

He shoved the door open. "Personal business."

As they entered the lab, Lila stared, wide-eyed, at the collection of satellite images on the screens around the room. Justin pointed out Afghanistan, Iraq, Pakistan and Indonesia before leading her to a lighted map of Mexico.

He handed her the pointer. "If you touch the screen with the pointer and then touch another spot twice quickly, the number of miles between the two distances will flash. Or I can switch it to minutes."

She held the pointer between two fingers. "Cool."

"If you press down on a point on the map, the name of the town will flash on the screen, or the name of the nearest town and the distance."

She caught her full lower lip between her teeth and studied the map. Talking to herself, she said, "Let's see, I got to the border at around eight o'clock, stopped for forty-five minutes in Loma Vista before that."

He leaned in, watching her pore over the map. Her musky scent, a combination of tangy salt and stale lilac, enfolded him, weaving a silky web around him. He stepped back to break the threads.

She needed to get home, back to her family and friends. He knew instinctively she had lots of friends. Her warmth would draw people to her, grateful to be included in the glow that floated around her like a cape. God, he was losing it.

She murmured, "I think the site is around this area. It's south of this little town, Loma Vista. Some dense foliage marked the spot. The rest of the way to Loma Vista was pretty bare."

Blinking his eyes, he focused on the map where she circled with the wand.

"I can't be absolutely sure until I see the place again. It was dark, and I was sleeping when we got there and terrified when I left."

Drawing in closer, he noted the general location but didn't write it down. He frowned. "Are you sure this is the place?"

She nodded. "I'm figuring it out by hours not miles, and I'm sure I stopped in Loma Vista and it took me another forty-five minutes to the border. Why?"

Scratching his chin, he said, "It seems kind of far from the border to be tunneling in. I expected something closer to the border itself."

He flipped a switch to erase the entire transaction. "At least it gives me a starting point."

Handing him the pointer, she asked, "Why didn't you tell your colleagues out there about the tunnel?"

He shrugged. "It's only a supposition right now. Something Chad and I worked on, nobody else, except Molina, and I'm not sure how far Chad took him into his confidence."

She sighed. "I thought government agencies were supposed to be working together now—"

"Shh." He held up his hand.

She started to speak, and he hissed, "Quiet."

A hollow puff. A soft thud. A quick footstep.

He prowled toward the door of the navigation room, lifted a chair and lodged it under the door handle.

Her eyes round with fear, a sickly pallor soaking into her skin, Lila choked out, "What's wrong?"

He spun toward her, regretting his next words. "The facility's been compromised."

Chapter Three

A shot of adrenaline zigzagged up Lila's spine, leaving a trail of goose bumps in its wake. The blood pounded in her head. She squeezed her eyelids shut against the daggerlike pain that knifed behind them.

Justin gripped her shoulders and her eyes flew open. She twitched then sagged against him. He pressed her body to his, the warmth quelling the panic that rippled along her nerve endings.

Through their clothes, she felt his hard muscles already coiled for action. In contrast, she felt like jelly. If he let her go, she'd morph into a blob on the floor.

He looked down into her face, and she tried to soak up the strength she saw in his eyes. He ran his palms down her arms and squeezed her hands. "Follow me."

His touch and words acted like an electric prod. She straightened up. The room sharpened into focus. Her nostrils flared. Her muscles tensed. She could do this.

Before grabbing her wrist, Justin swung around and killed the lights. He prowled across the floor, the satellite images casting a green glow over his taut body. He placed a chair beneath a vent, climbed on it and pushed the vent into the ceiling above them.

He beckoned to her to join him on the chair, and she teetered on its edge. Encircling her waist with his strong hands, he hoisted her up and into the vent.

He whispered, "Crawl to your right until you get to a dead end. I'll be right behind you."

Turning toward the blackness, she heard him scramble into the vent after her. She began crawling, her breath puffing out in short spurts, scattering the cobwebs tickling her face. The dark enclosure suffocated her, but she kept moving, afraid if she stopped, she'd die. Her head hit a wall. She gulped once, twice, to swallow the scream barreling its way up her throat.

Justin crowded in close to her, sweat dripping from his face. His hot breath, smelling of cool spearmint, bathed her cheek. He lifted out another vent and lowered himself through the square hole. As he disappeared, waves of panic engulfed her until she saw his face peering up at her.

He said, "Come down."

She sat down on the edge of the hole and dangled her legs through the opening. Fear drummed against her temples until Justin wrapped his arms around her thighs. She slid down the rest of the way, and he held her close for just a moment. Could she stay here… forever? His heart thudded against her chest, willing her own skittering heart to mimic its steady beat.

His lips brushing her ear, he said, "We're in a closet in the entryway. The front door is right outside. Do what I say. Once I open the front door, crouch down as far as you can and follow me out to the car. Don't look up, don't stop. The keys are in the ignition. If I don't make it…"

Her strangled cry stopped him. He moved his hands up her arms to cup her face and swept the rough pad of his thumb across her lips. He dropped one hand and dug into his pocket. "If I don't make it, call the number on this card and ask for Leo Caine." He nudged the card into her stiff, damp hand.

Wrapping his finger around one of her curls, he bent over and pulled her face toward his, his lips brushing hers. "You can do it, Lila."

Couldn't they just stay in this closet and finish the kiss? All too soon, he released her, prepared his weapon and eased the closet door open. She peered out from behind his broad back. No one in the entryway. Two steps put them at the front door.

Pushing it open, he glanced back at her. "Let's go."

He hunched forward, folding his tall frame almost in half. She followed, her eyes darting around the perimeter of the compound.

The first shot split the hot desert air.

Following orders, she didn't look up.

Justin moved faster, not bothering to return fire. Another shot. He dropped.

She stumbled over him. Just a few feet ahead, the car beckoned, promising safety.

Shoving her forward, he yelled, "Go."

She took a few steps and then turned to see him gripping his leg, blood flowing between his fingers. "You're hurt."

He shouted, "Go, I can't get up. It's my leg."

She charged back, stooping over and hooking him

under the arms. "Move, damn you. You can't leave me now."

She felt a surge of power jolt his body as he staggered onto his good leg. She yanked open the door on the side away from the gunfire and pushed him into the car. He slumped against the seat, still holding his leg, and she scrambled over him to the driver's seat.

A bullet smacked behind them, and a spiderweb of shattered glass spread across the back window. She punched the truck forward.

Speeding toward the closed gate, she screamed, "The gate. How do I open the gate?"

He responded through clenched teeth. "Push the red button."

She pounded the button with her fist and the gates rolled open. The truck squealed through and raced back toward Highway 62. Away from the compound. Away from terror. Toward the unknown.

For several miles, ragged breathing and choked sobs filled the car until Justin swore softly and bent forward.

Lila glanced over, her eyes dropping to his thigh. Blood oozed through ripped denim. "Is it bad?"

He grimaced before answering. "It's not too bad. Grazed me. Bullet didn't go in."

He peeled his T-shirt off his back and wound it around his leg.

Lila frowned. "You're going to need better treatment than that."

His lips tight, outlined in white, he pressed down on the makeshift bandage with two hands. "Can't go to a doctor. I have a first aid-kit in the truck bed."

Watching the blood seep through his T-shirt, she

asked, "What just happened back there? How'd you know?"

Leaning back, he closed his eyes. "I heard some noises. A silencer."

She stared hard at the road. "Who was it? Weren't there just the seven of us at the compound?"

Feeling him tense beside her, she glanced over at him. He seemed chiseled in stone, his face etched into hard lines, the muscles in his bare chest and belly tight.

He grunted and answered, "That's what worries me."

"Y-you mean…?"

"I mean, it looks like an inside job. Dig into my pocket and get my phone for me."

He shifted his hip so she could reach his front pocket. Keeping her eyes on the highway, her fingers skimmed the smooth skin above the waistband of his jeans, dancing over his hipbone to reach his pocket. The heat of her blood owed nothing to the ball of fire dropping into the desert. The warmth suffused her cheeks as she handed him the phone. If he noticed her blush, he gave no sign. Of course not, the man had the emotions of a robot.

He punched a few keys to speed dial a number and barked into the phone, "Leo, it's Justin." Pause. "Cut the code-name crap. The compound's been hit."

Lila heard only his side of the conversation, but it didn't seem to be going well. When he finished, he dropped the phone and clamped down on his thigh with both hands again. He glared in front of him, his eyebrows drawn together.

She licked her lips. "Is there a problem?"

"Yeah, Leo said Prasad never called him with the

news about Chad's death. He didn't know a thing about it…or you."

Her mouth dropped open. "Prasad?"

Hunching one bare shoulder, he said, "I don't know. Don't even know if he left before the shooting started. We were in there for a good forty-five minutes before I heard the first bullet. If he already left, he's still alive somewhere. If he didn't, he's dead like the rest or…"

Recalling the young agent's open face and engaging smile, Lila shook her head. Couldn't be. "Could it be someone from the outside? Honestly, the security didn't seem that tight there."

He shrugged. "I suppose. I didn't notice any other cars there, but then we usually park them around the back of the compound. I didn't notice if Prasad's car was still there or not, either."

"Where to now? Can we go see this Leo?"

"No."

She swiveled her head to look at him. "Why not?"

He gave a harsh laugh. "From the sound of his voice and the things he didn't say, I can tell he's suspicious… of me."

She exclaimed, "Of you? He thinks you opened fire on those people?"

"I'm still standing." He adjusted the T-shirt on his thigh, his jaw tight. "Process of elimination."

"That's ridiculous. You're the one who called the incident in. Couldn't you just explain the situation to him?"

Shaking his head, he said, "Not if he thinks I'm involved. There'd be an investigation, they'd take my weapon. I'd be useless in following up on anything Chad found. I'm not too good at being useless."

She eyed the contained energy in that hard body and could easily believe it.

"Look, Lila. It's better to stay out of sight for now. I need to sort some things out in my head."

"Better for whom?" she asked. "You need to rest and have that wound properly cleaned and dressed. I need to eat, and I'm sorry, I really need a shower."

His grin ended in a gasp as he clutched at his thigh again. "I have camping gear in the back and that first-aid kit. That's probably the safest way to go right now. I've been checking the mirror since we left the compound. Nobody followed us. That's one advantage of the desert. You can see for miles. It's no accident the HIA put the compound out here."

She announced, "Okay. We're going to stop at that shopping center when we get to Twentynine Palms. I'm going to pick up a few things, and then we're going camping."

An hour later they sat on logs around a fire at the Cottonwood campsite in the Joshua Tree National Park. Justin looked over at the woman poking at the flames. She amazed him. Instead of making her swoon, the sight of his blood bubbling through his jeans called her to action. For a moment at the compound he thought he'd have to haul her out over his shoulder. For a moment.

With little assistance from him, she pitched the tent, treated his gunshot graze and started a fire, humming a tune all the while.

While she cleaned and dressed his wound, her strong, nimble fingers trailing over his skin stirred a slow burn in the pit of his stomach. He didn't need this complication right now.

The blaze from the campfire illuminated her fine features. She looked like an escaped wood nymph from the Black Forest, but her coloring resembled one of those Nordic heroines.

Noticing his scrutiny, she smiled, but those lush lips quivered with the effort. She plucked up stamina from somewhere to keep going, but the path to total collapse loomed ahead. He hoped to God he could catch her when she folded.

Against his better judgment, he shifted a little closer to her. "What kind of research were you doing in Mexico?"

She clasped her hands around her knees and rocked back and forth. "A group of us went down to dive and do research at La Bufadora. There's a decline in the fluorescent strawberry anemone there, and we're testing the water for toxins."

His eyebrows shot up. "Strawberry what?"

Wiggling her toes at the fire, she laughed. "The fluorescent strawberry anemone. I swear, that's what it's called. We drove down in a caravan, and I decided to leave early. My car broke down, and the rest is history."

Obviously she took life head-on, no shrinking violet, despite her ethereal appearance. "So as a graduate student, do you teach, too?"

She nodded and grimaced. "I spend half my time doing research and the other half as a teaching assistant in undergraduate marine-biology classes."

"Have you always been interested in marine biology?"

She laughed again, the sound of gurgling water. "Is that your polite way of asking why a woman of my advanced years is still in school?"

He tilted his head, taking in the large, clear eyes set in a smooth face, a sprinkling of freckles across her nose.. "I'd hardly call late twenties *advanced*."

She leaned forward and winked. "Must be good genes. More like early thirties, and no, while marine biology is my first love, I made a detour for a while."

Closing her eyes, a spasm of pain arched across her face. As much as he wanted to learn more about her, he respected others' private demons. After all, he had his share.

She opened her eyes. "How about you? Did you want to be a secret agent when you were a little boy?"

The reference to his boyhood pinked his armor. He'd just wanted to survive his childhood, make it out in one piece. He schooled his face into a noncommittal mask. "Not exactly. I wanted to be a cowboy, then an astronaut, then a superhero."

Nodding, she said, "I see, the quiet life. I know someone poured from the same mold." Her expressive eyes misted over as she stared dreamily into the fire.

The blaze crackled, and she fell back to earth. "When can I go home?"

He stirred the fire with a stick. "When I can get you there safely. If all goes well tonight, maybe as early as tomorrow."

Leaning toward him, she asked, "Do you really think Prasad could be responsible for what happened at headquarters?"

He pictured Prasad's eager young face as he told him, "I have more at stake here than you. I'm an American and I'm a Muslim." His background check came back squeaky clean. Justin himself trained him…and Chad.

Nausea swept through his body, and he gripped his hands in front of him. That's what happened when you got too close—betrayal or desertion.

"Justin?"

He looked over at that angelic face, her hair creating a halo that seemed to float around her head.

She reached out and touched his clasped hands. Her warmth spread through him like honey, sweet and thick, and he savored it. Just for this one moment…

Her fingertips played along the grooves between his knuckles. She felt his tension begin to seep out, and she let it bleed into her, drinking in their closeness. He had to feel their connection, too. Or maybe not.

He stood up slowly. "You must be exhausted. Time for that shower."

He began dousing the fire, and she jumped up to help him. The man obviously could tolerate only small doses of intimacy at a time.

When they finished, she asked, "What will you do?"

He rubbed his hand across the stubble that made him look nine kinds of sexy. "Probably go down to that clearing south of Loma Vista."

She widened her eyes, and her heart skipped. "Alone? You'll go down there without any help?"

"Much of what we do in this agency is alone. Besides, we do have another agent down there."

She guessed much of what *he* did in the agency was alone. Lone Wolf—he'd earned that name somehow.

"One more thing, Lila, you can't tell anyone about this. The police agencies don't even know about us. The government will take care of that incident at the compound."

"What about Chad's family?"

"They're back East. They'll be notified."

"And the rest of them?"

"Same thing."

She shivered thinking about the elegant Victoria and nerdy Dave. Real people with real families. She asked, "What about your family?"

His body stiffened, dark clouds scudding across his face. "Don't have one, except for my sister. She's married and thinks I have some government job where I travel a lot. Not too far from the truth."

He gestured toward the squat building beyond the rocks. "You shower first, and I'll wait outside."

The Cottonwood campground consisted of forty campsites and ten shower complexes. They enjoyed this one to themselves, as the late-summer months didn't attract many campers to the desert.

Lila tiptoed into the empty building that housed four shower stalls and cranked on the lukewarm water. The spray hit her back, and she soaped up her body, scrubbing away the sand and dust along with her tension and fear.

Justin stood guard outside, and after knowing him less than twenty-four hours, she knew he'd protect her. He seemed to believe they might be safe now. God, she hoped so. She ached to see Tyler again and hold him in her arms.

She toweled off and called out to Justin to make sure he was still stationed out front. He answered her call. She'd marveled at the supplies in his truck, like the soap and this towel. He lived prepared for flight. A strange, rootless existence.

She dragged her shorts and tank top back over her clean body and stepped outside. She grinned at Justin leaning against a boulder. "Better hurry. I think I used up all the hot water."

He shoved off the rock. "Hold this gun, just in case. I'll have mine, too. If you hear or see anything, come into the shower."

She gave him her best wicked smile. "I might just use that as an excuse."

His eyes burned with an amber light, as if daring her to make her move. Then he shook his head and ducked into the little building.

Silence hung over the campground, punctuated by the sound of metal on metal as someone at a distant site secured his tent. A shuffling noise rose from behind a rock on the other side of the shower building. Lila's eyes darted to the rock formation looming at the edge of the shadows. The bush rustled and swayed. An animal?

She raised the trembling gun and pointed at the bush. Her voice scissored through the heavy air. "Justin."

He got out of the shower as fast as he could with his bad leg, tucking the ends of the towel around his waist with one hand and gripping his gun with the other. "What's wrong?"

She pointed to the rocks. "I heard a rustling noise by the bush over there."

"Stay here…and put that gun down." He prowled toward the outcropping. Raising his weapon, he crept around the rock. Lila covered her ears to block out the…silence.

He returned to her side. "Probably just a small animal. Admit it. You made it up to lure me out here."

Her heart, returning to its normal number of beats per minute, sped up again at the sight of his naked body strategically wrapped in the small towel. The water from the shower glistened on his broad shoulders, the droplets shimmering in the hair scattered across his well-defined chest. His dark brown hair, sluiced back from his face, curled up where the ends met the nape of his neck. An aching need poured into her with such force, she stepped back.

Her inventory finished, she looked up into his eyes. She glimpsed her own desire mirrored there before the shutters came down.

He turned quickly to the shower. "I'll finish up."

By the time he returned, she'd marshaled her reeling senses. This kind of attraction to this kind of man couldn't happen. They walked slowly back to the campsite, a multitude of brilliants winking down at them from the black velvet canvas above.

He peeled back the flap of the tent and reached into his bag. Handing her one of his T-shirts, he said, "Get out of those clothes and put this on unless you have something cleaner to wear to bed."

She accepted the T-shirt. "I haven't done laundry since that last hotel in Ensenada."

He left her in the tent while she changed. She stripped off her shorts and tank top, unhooked her bra and dropped it on the pile of clothes. Pulling his T-shirt over her head, she wrapped her arms around herself, inhaling the clean scent of laundry detergent. She slipped into the sleeping bag and called out, "I'm ready."

He ducked into the tent, yanked his shirt off and

stepped out of the shorts he put on to replace the jeans with the bullet hole in the thigh. She'd already seen his boxers once today when she helped him out of his blood-soaked jeans and cleaned his wound. So why did her toes curl now?

His heavily muscled thigh had escaped with a nasty rip in the flesh, not much more. He had a comprehensive first-aid kit, and she had some training from Mom.

She schooled her eyes away from him as he crawled into his sleeping bag. He had so much to give and yet he shut himself down, sealing a tight lid on his emotions. What torments nagged him and drove him to keep vigil over his loneliness? And why did she care so much?

"Lila?" His voice caressed her like a warm embrace.

"Yeah?" Her pulse quickened.

"Good night, Lila."

She rolled onto her side in her cocoon, folding her arm beneath her head for a cushion. She screwed her eyes shut. She clenched her fists at every pop from the dying campfire, every time some misdirected insect beat its wings against the tent. Her fingernails dug half-moons into her palms. She shifted to her other side. As her eyes adjusted to the gloom, she spied Justin propped up in his sleeping bag.

She whispered, "Justin?"

"Yeah?"

"Aren't you going to sleep?" He had to be as exhausted as she was, and he had a nasty wound in the bargain.

"I'm going to keep watch for a while. Go back to sleep."

"I haven't been too successful in that endeavor." She continued, choosing her words, "Can I…?"

He answered by tugging on her sleeping bag, pulling it toward his own. Placing an arm around her shoulders, he guided her head onto his lap.

She settled her cheek against his good thigh, encased in the down of his sleeping bag, and drank in his fresh masculine scent, so different from Gareth's expensive colognes.

One strong, capable hand rested on her shoulder, and she felt safer than she had in the past twenty-four hours. She nestled her head deeper onto his lap, a long sigh escaping her lips. Safer than she'd ever felt before.

Lila's breathing deepened. The soft curves in her sleeping bag rose and fell rhythmically. He caressed her shoulder before allowing his fingers to swim in the sea of curls that rested in the hollow of her neck. He twisted them round and round until they bound him to her.

When he'd come out of the shower in that towel, the clear blue light of her eyes had muted into a smoldering need. A groan rumbled from his lips. He'd had the same need. He'd hastened a retreat to the shower before she could see just how much. His potent desire hardened and rose, then as now. He shifted in his sleeping bag. He was no better than Chad.

What had Chad meant to her? His death pained her, but then she seemed to feel everything acutely, both sorrow and joy. Chad had a way with women. Did Lila realize he had that effect on all women and used it liberally? Didn't matter now. Chad was gone.

He closed his eyes against his loss. His mother was all but gone. He wished his father would stay gone, the son of a bitch. And soon Lila would be gone. He preferred it that way.

His thigh throbbed, and suddenly feeling pinpricks of heat, he kicked the sleeping bag off his leg.

Lila mumbled something in her sleep, sounded like "tired." Well, she should be after the horrors she'd witnessed over the past twenty-four hours. He still couldn't quite understand what possessed Chad to bring her along when he knew danger loomed ahead. The kid always had to have a backup plan.

Justin tried recalling their last conversation. Chad's excitement fizzed in his voice when he said, "I met up with some coyotes here in Mexico City. They told me about a tunnel running under the border, but it's not finished yet. I'm sure our boys with Al Tariq are following the same leads. We have to find it before they do."

They both knew what a tunnel under the border meant—easy access for terrorists to slip into the country undetected. It would be a free-flowing pipeline resulting in thousands of terrorist cells right in their own backyard.

Justin told him to wait until he finished his personal business in San Diego and could join him. The hothead didn't wait. Did he learn that from him?

And what happened to Molina? Did he know about Chad yet? Why did he run off to Costa Rica? Chad hadn't trusted him. He'd told him flat out he wouldn't work with Molina until Justin got down there.

This situation would've been a mess even if Chad hadn't dragged Lila into their business. Now their entire operation was a disaster.

He gazed down at her, tracing his finger along her earlobe. Soft as silk. He'd drink her in tonight and set her free tomorrow.

The silence of the campsite didn't fool him. Every nerve ending in his body tuned into a waiting presence in the crouching darkness. He didn't know what that presence waited for, or why it didn't strike. But when it did, he'd be ready.

He was born ready.

Chapter Four

Rivulets of sweat stung his eyes. He clenched his jaw against the chills that threatened to claim his body.

Lila rustled beside him. Brushing her hand across her face, she rolled her head off his lap. Lids still at half-mast, she murmured, "What time is it?"

"Seven o'clock." Justin stifled a moan.

She blinked a few times and sat up, her sleeping bag falling off her shoulders. She cocked her head at him. "Your eyes are glassy."

Reaching out, she trailed her cool fingertips along his forehead. "You're burning up, Justin. I was afraid those antibiotics with the expired date might not work."

He muttered through sandpaper lips, "No doctors."

She shoved off the rest of her sleeping bag and tugged at his T-shirt bunched up around her waist. Not before he caught sight of one silky thigh as it rounded into her hip. He closed his eyes. He didn't need to get any hotter.

Leaning over him, she folded her arms and demanded, "Have you been awake all night?"

He dipped his head. "Had to keep watch."

Her eyes narrowed. "I thought you said nobody followed us."

A shiver snaked its way through his body, and he hunched his shoulders to ward it off. "Don't think anyone did."

Her eyes tracked his every movement. "This conversation is wearing you out. Lie down. I'll get you some water and more ibuprofen. Then we pack up and leave."

He shifted, raising his arm.

She said, "Don't worry. I'll take that other gun with me."

Turning her back on him, she yanked the T-shirt over her head. Through half-closed eyes, he watched her. Couldn't turn away. Crisscross tan lines from a one-piece swimsuit marked her shoulders and back. Her bikini panties hugged her just below the curve of her hip.

His temperature notched up a few degrees, and it had nothing to do with the fever.

She finished dressing, got him the water and packed up camp. As they peeled out of Cottonwood, he kept his eye on the mirror. All clear.

Now it was his turn to ask, "Where are we going?"

"Santa Barbara, if you can hold on."

"Santa Barbara? What's in Santa Barbara?"

She grinned. "My mom."

He lifted his eyebrows, and she answered, "She's a nurse."

On the four-hour drive to Santa Barbara, strands of doubt threaded through the confusion of his mind. If Prasad was the traitor, he didn't know Lila's full name, and she was still safe.

Would he even want to harm her now? It's not as though she could identify anyone, and they must already know the location of the tunnel. They were lying in wait for Chad. They must've realized his informant met him there to show him the tunnel. Didn't they?

The location of the tunnel puzzled him. If the tunnel started in Loma Vista, as Lila suggested, that would be one hell of a tunnel to the border.

He shook his head. If they already found the tunnel, why shoot at Lila? Even if she went to the police, Prasad would know the police wouldn't conduct a thorough investigation into the matter. An American in Mexico, possibly involved in drug or people smuggling, killed? No. A nonissue.

He stopped. They shot at him, too. Did Prasad realize she'd come straight to him? She insisted nobody followed her. Maybe Prasad dispatched his accomplices to his house knowing she'd eventually show up there.

Lila's knowledge of the tunnel didn't threaten them. An HIA agent having the same knowledge did.

Her very proximity to him endangered her life. They wanted to kill him, not her. He'd leave her in Santa Barbara and work through the rest of this mess on his own.

He couldn't come in until he figured out who betrayed them, but he didn't blame Leo for suspecting him. Start with the obvious—the ones still alive. But once the HIA started investigating him, he'd never get to that tunnel. Months of hard work and Chad's death would mean nothing. He couldn't allow that to happen. Wouldn't allow that to happen. He'd get justice for Chad if it killed him.

Lila turned up the radio and sang along to the song. She knew every word, bobbing her head to the rhythm.

He snorted to himself. So much for his instincts about people. She'd fooled him. He'd pegged her for a scatterbrained, airhead. But that delicate golden beauty and those wide blue eyes masked a woman of guts and heart.

She stopped singing. "You awake?"

"I've been awake. Just thinking."

"Figure anything out yet?"

He nodded. "I have a theory anyway."

She waited.

He sighed. "Prasad ratted out Chad to his associates in Mexico. They followed Chad, and you, to the location of the tunnel and killed him and his informant. He led them right to it. They didn't follow you because they couldn't. The Mexicans either killed them or delayed them. Prasad either had his associates pick you up at the border and follow you, or he figured you'd come straight to me anyway. Maybe he thinks Chad already told me about the tunnel. It's me they want. They don't care if you know about the tunnel."

He inclined his head in apology. "Nobody's going to take your story seriously."

She stuck a pink tongue out at him and he laughed. "Sorry. They're not concerned about you. They don't want me or the rest of HIA to know about it."

She wrinkled her nose. "What about the guy in the trunk?"

Rubbing his hand across the stubble that was fast becoming a beard, he said, "I think he was Chad's contact, the one who showed him the location of the tunnel. The terrorists ambushed them, killed the informant first, stowed him in the trunk and then went to work on Chad."

"Justin, why didn't you just tell Leo about the tunnel or everyone at HIA yesterday? If you spread the word, Prasad's going to have to kill a lot of people."

He squinted out the window and answered, "I don't know. Instinct. You learn to play it close to the vest in this business."

"Chad was careless, wasn't he?"

"He was a damn good agent, but he had his weaknesses. We all do."

She coughed. "Women?"

Avoiding her eyes, he said, "On occasion." He didn't want to hurt her, especially if Chad had seduced her. The thought had him clenching his fists.

"Yeah, I could tell."

"Could you?" He studied his bandage, hoping she wasn't going to cry.

She snorted. "He flirted with every pretty woman up the coast of Baja."

"That didn't bother you?" He wrinkled his brow.

Turning to stare at him, she asked, "Why should it?"

As he gaped and stuttered, her eyes kindled with a blue blaze.

She hissed, "You think I slept with Chad? You think I fell for him so hard I'd do anything for him?"

He held up his hands, his relief so great he could bear the stings of her anger. "I'm sorry. I know Chad's reputation with the ladies. I just assumed…"

She pursed her lips before answering, "You assumed wrong."

He slumped back in his seat. He'd been wrong about

her, but if she hadn't fallen hard for Chad, why'd she risk so much to help him? The woman puzzled him as much as this tunnel.

She studied him for a moment. "You look better. Feeling better?"

He pinched his soaking T-shirt away from his chest and let it snap back. "Fever broke."

She nodded and started singing again, and he crossed his arms over his chest. At least one fever broke. And he'd have to work on the other one.

They drove through downtown Santa Barbara and up State Street amid the waving palms. The car kept climbing up the hills, the Pacific Ocean shining through the gaps. Her mom must be loaded.

They meandered up a long drive where the houses sat surrounded by land. Up the next rise, a low, rambling Spanish-style home appeared, all Mexican tiles and arches.

She wheeled the truck around the circular driveway and parked behind a white van.

Lila swung open the carved double doors, and as they entered a cool, dark hallway, she called out, "Mom, Ty? Anyone home?"

A clicking of heels announced a slender woman with gleaming hair swept up from high cheekbones.

Her gray eyes widened. "Lila. What are you doing here?" Her delicate hands fluttered at her breast, and she hung back.

Justin's eyes immediately darted around the hallway, examining every entrance, senses alert. Something was wrong. The woman, obviously Lila's mother, quivered with nervous energy.

Lila broke away from him and hugged the woman. "I got back from Mexico a little early." She gestured toward Justin and said, "This is—"

She stopped. He gave her a nod, and she continued, "Justin Vidal."

After the introductions, Lila's mother, Robbie Monroe, looked down at Justin's bandaged thigh. "What happened?"

Lila answered, "It's a gunshot wound. I did the best I could, but he took expired antibiotics and he developed a fever last night. Can you help him?"

Robbie stepped back, her face creased with worry.

Rubbing Robbie's arm, Lila explained, "I ran into a little trouble in Mexico, Mom."

Her mother groaned. "Not again."

Lila rushed in. "No. Nothing like that."

Justin looked at her sharply, but she avoided his gaze.

She gave her mother just enough of the story to make it sound unbelievable and absurd to Justin's ears, but her mother accepted it with a shrug.

"Let's make Justin comfortable. I have some penicillin, and I'll put a clean bandage on the wound and check it for infection."

As Robbie worked over him, Lila kept glancing toward the two entrances to the great room. "Where's Tyler?"

Again she avoided Justin's eyes. He ground his teeth together. If she had a husband waiting in the wings, she should've told him. He stopped the course of his proprietary thoughts. She didn't owe him any explanations.

Lila planted herself in front of Robbie, whose hands started to tremble as she finished Justin's bandage.

"Tell me, Mom."

Robbie concentrated on putting the gauze and tape back into her first-aid kit. "It's Gareth. He picked up Tyler two days ago. Decided he didn't want him to spend the whole month here after all and exercised his custody rights."

"He's supposed to have him two weekends out of the month. This isn't a weekend."

Robbie shrugged. "He knew you were on a research trip and just took advantage of the situation."

Lila sank back down to her chair, her face in her hands. Her head shot up. Justin expected tears, but her eyes glittered with something else. "What did he say this time?"

Robbie sighed. "Same old thing. He wants the money back."

Justin cleared his throat. "Lila, do you want to tell me what the hell is going on?"

Robbie heaved herself up from her crouching position. "I'll get you two something to eat."

When Robbie exited, silence loomed over the room.

Justin leveled a gaze at Lila. "Well?"

She expelled a long breath. "Tyler's my son, and Gareth's my ex-husband."

Although he figured as much from the previous conversation, her words dropped on him like stones. "Why didn't you tell me this before?"

Her chin jutted forward. "Why would I?"

Because he thought he had a corner on all the secrets. He'd come to expect honesty from her. "You didn't think the fact that you have a son was important?"

She answered, "It is important. That's why I kept it to myself. I figured he'd be safer that way, which is why I'm leaving him with Gareth for now."

He rolled his eyes, his earlier opinion of her as a ditz surging back. "Does your ex-husband always take him when you're gone?"

She answered, "You really want to hear this? It has nothing to do with our…your current predicament."

Looking at her face creased with worry, he did want to hear it. He wanted to smooth away the pain and anger that lingered in her eyes. He wanted to restore that evanescent aura that danced around her, making everything better for everyone, making the world less bleak.

He said, "I really want to hear it."

She sighed. Staring out the window to the ocean in the distance, she began. "I have primary custody of my son. Gareth gets a few weekends a month with him. Didn't want him any more than that and rarely requests the weekends he does have."

The pain that floated somewhere deep inside him at all times surfaced and grabbed his gut. "I understand."

That earned him a quizzical look. "He does, however, want money, my money."

He asked, "Wasn't that all worked out in the divorce settlement? He's not even willing to pay alimony or child support?"

Her lips lifted in a half smile. "It's more than that, Justin. I walked away from that marriage with millions."

He stared at her for a moment, and then spread his arms out to encompass the lofty great room, the spacious house and the view of the Pacific. "Is this yours?"

She dipped her head, hunching her shoulders. "Yeah, it's all mine. I bought it for Mom two years ago."

Justin drew in his breath. "So your husband's rich

and had to give you half of everything he owned as part of the divorce settlement."

"Something like that." Her lashes descended over her eyes.

She stunk as a liar, but he let it go. "How can he make you give him money by withholding your son if it's all laid out in the agreement?"

She chewed on her lip and looked down.

Robbie entered the room carrying a tray with iced tea and glasses. "Tell him, Lila. You have nothing to be ashamed about."

"I have a criminal record."

The golden girl had a criminal record? How many more surprises did she have stashed away?

Placing the tray down on the coffee table within Justin's reach, Robbie said, "The district attorney reduced the charges to one misdemeanor count. I don't see how Gareth can use that."

Lila glanced up at Justin through her lowered lashes. "I got into a little trouble several years back, and Gareth's threatening to use it against me in a custody fight over Tyler unless I cough up the money."

Justin growled, "Sounds like a great guy. How'd you ever wind up with him, Lila?" But he already knew. She had a thing for lost causes. Did she consider him one of those?

She grimaced. "He changed. Money changed him."

Robbie patted her daughter's arm. "It didn't change you, except to give you the means to squander it on me and Matt. And Tyler, of course."

Justin drew in a breath. Another man in her life? "Who's Matt?"

Lila grabbed a framed photo from the bookcase behind the sofa and dropped it in his lap. "My brother."

A young man with long shaggy blond hair and a surfboard under one arm gazed at the ocean. Her allegiance to Chad crystallized, as he and her brother could be twins. "He's a surfer?"

She took the frame from him and polished it with the edge of her T-shirt. "He used to be a professional surfer until his accident. He broke his neck in Australia, and he's in a physical-therapy center now."

Robbie sighed. "It's a very expensive place. I could have him here."

Lila said sharply, "That's too much work for you, Mom."

Robbie winked. "She just doesn't trust me. Thinks she has to handle every problem on her own. Thinks only she has the power to save the world and all its creatures."

"Please. Justin's not interested in that."

"He should know what he's up against. You two finish the lunch." She wrinkled her nose. "And you need a shower and some clean clothes."

Lila smiled. "Don't worry, that's my plan."

When her mother withdrew from the room, Lila's smile turned into a frown. "Matt's doctors say there's no physical reason why he can't walk. He's just given up."

Justin drained his iced tea and poured another glass. Families. Couldn't live with them and…couldn't live with them. "So tell me what kind of trouble you were in."

She poked at the ice in her glass with her finger. "You already think I'm a naive idiot."

He put down his glass. "Did I say that?"

"No, but sometimes I can see it in your eyes."

He'd have to be more careful. Nobody ever accused him of being easy to read before. "I hope I've shown nothing but admiration for the way you've handled yourself these past two days. You saved my life outside the HIA compound and I never even thanked you."

She grinned. "Purely selfish reasons. I wouldn't have been able to make it out those gates without you."

"Somehow I doubt that. Tell me what happened before."

She drew a deep breath. "When I was in college, a boy-friend and I went to Hawaii together. When we flew back into San Diego, the authorities pulled us aside and checked our suitcases. They found several bags of marijuana."

"You didn't know?"

"No. I knew Adam had some problems with drugs, but with my help, he put that behind him, or so I thought. He stashed the weed in my suitcase after I packed it."

His hands fisted. "What happened?"

"They arrested us at the airport. My mom found a good attorney for me, and the D.A.'s office dropped the felony charges against me, although according to the terms of my agreement, I had to enter a drug-treatment program. I never even used drugs."

His brow furrowed. "Having that experience, you willingly followed Chad's instructions after seeing him murdered?"

She smiled. "I wasn't wrong about Chad."

"After going through that, how could you trust…?"

Tilting her head at him, she asked, "Trust what?

Anyone? Anything ever again? You can't go through life not trusting. Sure, sometimes people let you down, but sometimes they don't. And it's those times when they don't that make life worth living."

What a messy way to live. He shook his head. "Lila, you need to be more careful. You're too trusting."

She stood up. "I'm also in desperate need of a shower. That campground shower just didn't do the trick."

She left him resting on the couch, her mom's expert bandage protecting his wound. By the time she reached the staircase, he'd already closed his eyes.

She tripped up the rest of the steps. His amber eyes hadn't judged her when she told him the story. Was Justin warning her about him with that remark about being careful?

She decided on a bath instead of a shower and sank down into the lilac-scented bubbles.

It was coming to an end, her adventure. God, she should be happy. Terror, panic and stress had been her constant companions over the past forty-eight hours.

She saw a man murdered.

Found a dead body.

Lost a dead body.

She'd had people manhandle her, shoot at her and follow her. Why did she feel like crying now that it was all over? Justin Vidal.

She eased deeper into the tub, letting her hair float around her. She found the man incredibly sexy. No way around it. A pleasant tingle rose from her inner thighs to her breasts when she remembered the taut, smooth texture of his skin beneath her fingers. His body wet from the shower. The tight muscles of his belly that led down to…

She ducked under the water. He planned to leave her here and go away. He'd go back to chasing terrorists, and she'd rally her forces for another fight with Gareth.

This wouldn't be the first time Gareth played this hand. It angered her but didn't worry her. Tyler would be safe with his father. Gareth would ply him with expensive toys and electronic gadgets, never fully grasping that a ten-year-old boy's love couldn't be bought.

Ty would come home laden with his bribery gifts and return to his animals, his friends at school and his uncle's surfing videos. If Gareth wanted to force another confrontation over the money, she'd play along to get Ty back home. Then she'd hire an attorney and fight back.

She finished bathing and dressed in a light summer skirt and camisole. She perched on the edge of Ty's bed, hugging his stuffed lion. He'd protested when she'd tried to give his remaining stuffed animals to charity. He'd assured her he needed them to chuck at his friends in an animal war. But she'd caught him a few times sound asleep with the lion pulled close to his chest.

"You'll bring him back home?"

Justin filled the doorway of Ty's bedroom. His dark, wet hair curled up at the ends. His clean-shaven face strong and handsome. She swallowed hard to rein in her impulse to go to him and fold herself around him.

She tossed the lion aside. "Yeah. My ex has done this before. This time I'm going to call his bluff. He can bring it on. I'll meet him with the best damn attorney money can buy. His money."

"That's better."

"What about you?"

"I'm going to Mexico. I'm going to find that tunnel."

"And Prasad?"

His jaw tightened. "I can't prove yet he's the traitor."

"But you will?"

"There'll be an investigation of the incident at the compound. I'm sure HIA agents have already been out there sweeping the place. If there's evidence, they'll be on it."

She plucked at Ty's comforter. "When are you leaving?"

"Tomorrow."

"Your leg?"

"It's fine."

"And me?"

Closing his eyes, he raked his hands through his hair. "You'll be fine, too. Prasad only knows your first name. Not enough to find you. No way he, or anyone else, followed us out here."

"You're sure?"

He hesitated, and her heart galloped. If they had been followed, she'd led the bad guys right to her mom. For once she was glad Gareth had Tyler. "You're not sure."

He sat down next to her on the bed. His clean masculine scent enveloped her, and she wanted to lose herself in it…in him.

"I had a feeling last night at the campsite someone was watching us, but I'm sure nobody followed us here. They'll be after me anyway. They're worried I'll go straight to the tunnel and they want to stop me."

His words failed to curtail the dread drumming against her temples. *They'll be after me anyway.* She pictured Justin in Chad's place, hands secured behind his back, helpless. Oh, no, she could never imagine this man helpless. He'd take his own life before delivering it into the hands of terrorists.

The rough pad of his finger trailed along her jaw. "What are you thinking?"

She caught her breath and wondered how his lips would taste. A real kiss this time. She said, "You'll be in danger," *and there's nothing I can do to stop it.*

He dropped his hand from her face. "The story of my life."

His tawny eyes darkened as if a shadow passed over them. Gesturing around the room, he said, "Tell me about your son."

She laughed, nodding at the pictures and posters plastered to the walls. "As you can see, he loves baseball, especially the Padres. He has a photographic memory, and he's something of a math whiz, which he currently uses to calculate baseball stats."

He grinned. "At least he can't say math is useless, and it looks like the Padres might make a run for the World Series."

"Yeah, he's all over that since I promised him we'd go to the opening game, even if the Padres don't make it."

"He's a lucky kid to have a mom like you." A spasm of pain twisted his lips, and she folded her hands in her lap to suppress the urge to reach out to him. He must still feel the loss of his own mother.

"I'm lucky to have him, too. He's also crazy about surfing. He really admires Matt. If only Matt could find that in himself."

"He'll come around in his own time and his own way. You can't save everyone, Lila."

Her lips quivered in a smile. "You mean, I can't save the whole world?"

Shaking his head, he said, "Nobody can do that."

She retorted, "Not even Lone Wolf?"

"Especially not Lone Wolf." He pushed off the bed and strode to the window. "Is this really a ranch?"

She studied every detail of his body. The way his dark brown hair flipped up at the nape of his neck. His T-shirt stretched across his broad shoulders. Strong shoulders. His waist tapered to narrow hips. His muscular thighs flared out, one sporting a fresh bandage after his shower.

She rubbed her hands over her own thighs. She'd have to stop these ridiculous thoughts about him. He'd be gone tomorrow.

Remembering his question, she replied, "Not really, although Tyler keeps rabbits and guinea pigs and other rodents. I plan to get horses here someday and have Tyler learn how to ride, but I don't even ride myself. Would you like to take a walk around the grounds after dinner?"

He agreed and returned to the guest room to lie down and rest. Lila ran her hand over the indentation he left on the bed, caressing the folds of the bedspread.

Lone Wolf was a dangerous man, all right, and she wasn't thinking about terrorists.

Chapter Five

"The sunset from here is beautiful, really."

Justin stood close to Lila as they regarded the bleak cloudy sky that hung like a soggy blanket over the steely Pacific in the distance. He couldn't allow himself to get any closer. He had to end this.

He squinted into the haze, but the damp chill it threatened hadn't rolled inland yet. Or maybe the warmth of the woman beside him kept the cold at bay. Standing next to Lila kindled a slow blaze that started somewhere below his belly. That same fire threatened to overtake him as he sat next to her in her son's room. Her feminine scent, lilacs again, but this time sweet and fresh, tempted him into absurd flights of fancy.

He glanced into her laughing eyes. "I believe you. The view's spectacular anyway even without the grand finale. Are you cold?"

His eyes hungrily skimmed over her lithe body, soft and curvy in all the right places. The thin material of her camisole hugged the swell of her breasts, and he dragged his gaze away, swallowing hard.

Her pink cheeks and bright eyes told him he'd been

too obvious in his admiration of her assets. If his enemies found him this transparent, they'd have a field day.

She crossed her arms. "No, not yet. Wait until that fog sneaks up into the hills though. If and when it does, the temperature drops quickly."

He gestured toward the empty stables. "So when are you going to get those horses?"

"I'm not sure. I'd have to hire someone to look after them. I don't want to burden my mom any more than she already is."

Her mom hardly seemed burdened. Why did Lila feel the need to protect everyone? "Your father?"

"He worked as a motorcycle cop in San Diego. He died in an accident during a pursuit when I was ten. Matt was three."

"So your mom raised you alone? She never remarried?" That strength he witnessed seemed to be a family trait, at least among the women.

She jerked her head back and forth. "Oh God, no. She failed my father and couldn't stomach going another round with someone else."

That strong, capable woman in there didn't look as if she'd failed anyone…ever. "How'd she fail him?"

Lila's eyes narrowed and a surprising hardness edged her voice. "She didn't want him to be a cop. She used to badger him into quitting and becoming a salesman at her father's vitamin company. A salesman." She almost spit out the word.

Seems Lila reserved all her judgment for her mother and gave everyone else a pass. "That doesn't make her responsible for his death."

She shrugged and exhaled as her shoulders dropped.

"I didn't say she caused his death, but she did fail him. She should've been more supportive of his dreams, maybe then…"

"Maybe then?"

As if to brush the thought away, she waved her hands. "I shouldn't criticize my mom. The past is the past, and she's one tough cookie."

Her mother wasn't the only one. "Must run in the family."

"Mom has a shrine set up to my father in one of the rooms here. Care to take a tour?"

"I'll pass."

She laughed. "Smart decision."

He continued watching her, and she asked, "What? Do you think that's disrespectful? I can assure you, my dad would've found the shrine hilarious. He laughed at everything, even danger."

"It's not that. You have a rare talent, Lila."

She pursed her lips before replying. "Yeah, I know. For getting into trouble."

Obviously that ex-husband of hers drilled that into her head.

"No, for enjoying life. Every moment. For seeing the bright side of everything. It's a gift you give freely to others." *To me.*

She reached out and traced a line at the side of his mouth. Her touch scorched him. Capturing her hand, he pressed his lips against her palm, and she caressed the side of his face.

He placed his hand on the curve of her hip to steady himself against the current of electricity zinging through his body. She lifted her face to his, and he accepted the invitation, kissing her hard on the lips. Her mouth parted, and his tongue slid into her warmth.

He crushed her lips against his to imprint them on his memory. Moving his hand around to the small of her arched back, he swept her closer, and she responded by entwining her arms around his neck. His desire hardened, pressing against her. God, he could get lost here in this Shangri-la. Forget what he was and what he did for a living. Forget Chad's death. Forget Prasad's possible betrayal.

Pulling away from her lips and her arms and the gossamer web she'd been weaving about him from the moment she landed on his porch, he stepped back.

He felt as if he were emerging from a dream and rubbed his hand over his eyes to banish the fairy dust. "That was…"

She supplied, "Good?"

He shoved his hands in his pockets. "Not very wise."

"I've never been known for my wisdom," she retorted. "Ask anyone."

He moved away from her, away from the vortex that sucked him into her realm—a place where he lost all control. A dangerous place of unfettered emotions.

Looking down, she kicked at some pebbles. "Have you ever been married?"

"No. This line of work and marriage don't mix." There. He didn't want to hide anything from her. Didn't want her to think their attraction could lead to anything more.

She continued worrying the pebbles with the toe of her shoe. "Aren't any of the, uh…agents married?"

He counted on his fingers. "A few are." He thought

about Leo moving into administration to spend more time with his family, and Victoria's messy divorce, and Molina's girlfriend stewing in L.A. while he gallivanted around the world, leaving behind an ex-wife and a son he hardly knew.

"Just doesn't work." He tried to remind himself, as well as convince her.

She looked up. "Do they keep their spouses in the dark?"

Folding his arms, he said, "There's no policy in place for that. From what I understand, everyone handles it differently. It's like you leave the house in the morning with your business suit and briefcase, have a day like we did yesterday, and then return home. Your wife asks, 'How was your day, dear?' And you reply, 'Just swell, honey. I saved the world for democracy.' And she says, 'That's nice. Now, take out the trash.'"

She laughed, and he let the sound bubble over him. Maybe for the last time.

"I know what you do," she said, her large eyes searching his face.

"So you do." That kiss had been a big mistake, even though it felt anything but.

The chirp of his cell phone spared him from going any further down that path, a path choked with emotional weeds and debris.

He checked the display, frowned, and answered the call he'd been dreading. Walking away from Lila, he spoke quietly into the phone.

When he returned to her, she bit her lip. "Doesn't look like good news."

"It's not." He never got good news from that quarter.

"Is it Prasad? Is he the traitor?"

He looked away and pocketed his cell phone. "It's not about that. It's my mother."

Her voice rose. "Your mother? I thought your mother was dead."

His face stiffened as he went into lockdown mode. "I never told you that."

She faltered. "Y-you said your family was gone except for your sister. I assumed that meant…"

He cut her off, ice crackling around the edges of his voice. "You assumed wrong."

She flinched. "So she's not dead?"

His gaze returned to the mist creeping in from the coast, just beginning to swirl up the hills to blot out the remaining sunshine. A chill seeped into the air.

He snapped, "She might as well be dead. She's in a nursing home. She's ill."

Lila whispered, "I'm sorry."

"Don't be. Usually my sister handles any issues that come up with her, but she's on vacation with her family. That's why I had to come back from Mexico, just when Chad needed me most."

She spread her hands. "But your mother needs you, too."

"She doesn't need anyone, least of all me. She's beyond that. This is just another minor irritation I have to deal with before I go down to Mexico."

She jerked back as if he'd slapped her. "Like me? Am I a minor irritation, too?"

He held himself rigid, hating himself, hating the look in her eyes. Hurt. Betrayal. That's what happened when you got too close. He thought he'd learned that lesson. "Thanks for showing me around and… I'm leaving first thing tomorrow morning."

He strode away from her, back to the house. He clenched his fists, resisting the impulse, vibrating in every fiber of his being, to return to her side. Take her in his arms. Explain everything. Open himself up to her as he'd never opened himself up to anyone in his life.

Instead he kept putting one foot in front of the other. Best to get away while he still could. Leave her thinking he was a coldhearted bastard. The easy way out. The coward's way out.

When they'd kissed, he'd felt her body, soft, yielding, move against his. Her desire for him had echoed in her lips, reverberated in her fingertips, and he'd answered that call with a hungry passion of his own. But she didn't need him in her life. She had enough on her plate right now, and he'd suffered enough betrayal to lay himself open to any more.

The next morning he left. Robbie insisted on getting up early to prepare him breakfast. She re-dressed his wound, which was on the mend, and packed him a seven-day supply of antibiotics.

No sign of Lila.

As Robbie saw him to the door, he said, "Thanks for everything, Robbie. Don't let Lila do anything foolish to get Tyler back home."

Robbie put her hand on his arm. "Nobody has ever been able to stop Lila from acting on her feelings, except her father." Her eyes grew bright at the memory of the man who still loomed large in her life. Did she believe she'd failed her husband, or had Lila put that spin on it?

"She's like her father?"

She shook her head. "No, but they had a special bond. Jack enjoyed thrills and chills, Justin, and not just as part of his job. He raced cars, climbed mountains, jumped out of airplanes. Lila loved that excitement."

"It didn't terrify you?"

Pulling her sweater around her body, she hugged herself. "Of course it did. I nagged him to stop, but Lila thought she had some magic power to protect him."

"His death must've devastated her."

"You have no idea. She and my husband performed a ritual before he left for work every day. Just a silly series of kisses, one on the nose, one on the forehead, I can't remember now. The night before Jack died, Lila slept over at a friend's house, and Jack left for work before she came home. They missed their magic ritual, and he died."

God, no wonder she tried to rescue everyone. She had to make up for the one time she failed. He held out a scrap of paper. "Give this to Lila. Tell her to use it if she gets in trouble." He left off the "ever."

Robbie glanced down at his cell-phone number. "She just may need it."

He waved and walked down the driveway to his truck, its back window still shattered, reminding him of the task ahead. Turning to look at the house for the last time, he saw a curtain move in an upstairs room. Lila? He raised his hand, but the curtain fell back into place. The empty window glared back at him.

BY THE TIME Justin reached San Diego, he'd memorized every logical reason for forgetting about Lila. Recited each one in his head to convince himself to forget her. Her hair. Her lips.

He turned up the radio—loud.

He reached his street and drove slowly past his rental house. After circling the neighborhood a few more times, he pulled into his driveway. Looked clear. No one staking out the place.

His twin sister left him with a few things to bring their mother in the event the call came while she vacationed in Maui. A working vacation, since their deadbeat father contacted Kate with tales of remorse, redemption and sobriety. He snorted. Yeah, about twenty years too late.

He'd tried to stop Kate from going, wanted to protect her from any disappointment. She'd rejected his advice, claimed she didn't need protection from her own father. Since when?

Chad's car still squatted across the street, a green parking ticket fluttering under the windshield wiper.

As he approached the car to grab the ticket, his neighbor called out from his yard, "That your car?"

Justin stuffed the ticket in his pocket and opened the trunk. "No, friend of mine left it here. Had to leave suddenly."

The neighbor groused, "Well, if you don't move it, I'm having it towed. Damn piece of junk's an eyesore."

Justin assured him he'd move it. He wanted to do a more thorough search of the trunk anyway.

The neighbor asked, "You hear about that dead body?"

Justin froze. "What dead body?"

"A woman out walking her dog found a man's body dumped halfway down the slope of the canyon."

Keeping his voice steady, Justin asked, "Cops know who it is?"

The man shrugged. "Nah, some illegal by the looks of it. Mexican fellow. No ID."

"How'd he die?"

"Someone strangled him."

"When did it happen?"

Scratching his chin, the man answered, "Don't know, but the woman found the body yesterday. Day after those kids set off those firecrackers. Sure sounded like gunshots to me. Thought the two might be connected, but the body didn't have any gunshot wounds."

Justin buried himself in the trunk, saying over his shoulder, "Looks like I missed all the excitement."

He rummaged through the trunk. Could the body be Lila's dead guy? Chad's contact? The strangulation would explain the lack of any significant blood in the trunk.

Chad left one small bag in the trunk, and Justin dropped it on the ground. He ran his hands over the surface of the trunk, sand and dirt sticking to his palms.

Opening the back door, he spotted a rough blanket on the seat. Lila remembered being covered by a blanket. He raised it to his face and inhaled. Lilacs.

A sombrero and a donkey puppet lay on the front seat. Lila's? He grabbed the almost empty bottle of water from the cup holder. Brownish crystallized sediment floated at the bottom. He opened the bottle and sniffed. Gagging, he jerked the bottle away from his nose. Old gym socks. He held the bottle up to the sunlight, inspecting the brown crystals swirling in the liquid. Valerian root. Chad put Lila to sleep before pulling up to that clearing. Damn good thing he did.

Clapping the sombrero on his head, he gathered the rest of the car's contents and went inside. He needed more information about this dead body.

He punched in the number for Fletcher Bale, his contact at the San Diego Sheriff's Department. Fletch, Molina and he had all been recruited from other government agencies to become the first agents for the newly formed Homeland Intelligence Agency. Fletch resigned a few years ago, opting for marriage and family, or that's what he claimed.

"Bale here."

"Fletch, it's Vidal."

Fletch lowered his voice. "Whaddya got?"

He often gave Fletch leads on other crimes he ran across in the course of his own investigations. Fletch paid him back in kind.

Justin answered, "I'm hoping you can give me something this time."

"Shoot."

Justin took a deep breath. "What do you know about a dead body discovered in a canyon in the University City area?"

Fletch said, "Hold on. Let me bring it up on the computer."

A few clicks later, Fletch recited, "Illegal immigrant fresh over the border. Woman walking her dog found him. The dog went nuts when he got to the edge of the canyon."

Justin asked, "Time of death?"

"Let's see. No official autopsy back yet, but it's looking like two days ago. The woman found the body the following day. Some neighbors in the area reported hearing gunshots that morning, but he wasn't shot and those came in after the time of death."

"After?" The two men who shot at him and Lila must've pulled the body from the trunk and dumped it down the canyon. Why? The man was already dead, wasn't he? If not, Justin missed an opportunity to find out what he knew, including the location of the tunnel.

"That's right."

Justin continued, "Any evidence on the body?"

Fletch sighed. "Not much. The guy had some American money stuffed in his pocket. Doesn't look like robbery was a motive."

"What was?"

"Who knows. Argument with the coyote who brought him over maybe."

"You find anything else, Fletch?"

"Some unmatched fibers on his clothes. Couple of fresh oil stains."

Like from the trunk of a car? Justin swore.

"Okay, give it up, Vidal. You know something about this? What's your interest? You're not going to tell me this guy was a terrorist."

Justin said, "He is what he appears to be, an illegal immigrant who got caught up in a deadly game."

Fletch drew in a long breath. "That's the only kind you play. Are we going to find his killers?"

"You're not but I may just have a chance. Keep me posted, Fletch."

Justin ended the call, a crease lining his brow. Either the man in the trunk got out and wandered away to his death, or the guys who shot at him and Lila dragged him out to make sure he kept quiet. He must've been Chad's source on the tunnel. When Justin and Chad first went down there, they chased a rumor about a tunnel for the transport of illegal immigrants. Unfortunately, the terrorist group, Al Tariq, was following the same scent, hunting the same clues.

Did Chad and the man in the trunk have a meeting planned? Al Tariq either knew about the meeting or followed Chad. Maybe other coyotes, looking out for one of their own, attacked Chad's killers. Nausea punched his gut when he thought about those murderers inches away from Lila while she slept in the car.

Several things still didn't add up. If the tunnel was at the same location as the meeting, it was too far from the border. Had Chad been mistaken? How had Al Tariq made Chad? And if the original killers were dead or incapacitated and couldn't follow Lila, how'd Al Tariq wind up at his house? This smelled more and more like an inside job. God, don't let it be Prasad.

Thanks to Lila, he knew the general location of Chad's murder. He had to find it, find that tunnel, and destroy it before Al Tariq had a chance to use it for deadly purposes.

He glanced at the bag in the corner of the bare room. Damn. One more thing to take care of.

He drove north to Carlsbad and his unpleasant task. He winced recalling the distaste in Lila's eyes when he revealed his feelings about his mother. He couldn't help himself. Couldn't pretend she meant anything to him, not even for Lila.

Since the day his father deserted the family, his mother blamed Justin for that desertion. Constantly reminded him that he drove his father away. Blamed him for their lack of money. Blamed him for her loneliness. Blamed him for her "nerves," her euphemism for her drinking. She blamed it all on a fifteen-year-old boy.

He learned early that love put you in a vulnerable position. It gave others the power to hurt you, to betray you. Kate actually wanted him to go through that again?

Out of habit, he parked on the street outside the lush grounds of the nursing home instead of in the parking lot in the back. Didn't like to be hemmed in.

He jogged up the steps to the front door and presented himself to the attendant in the lobby.

"I'm here to see Marian Vidal."

The attendant frowned. "Is she expecting you?"

Placing the bag down, he said, "She should be. You called me. Some crisis?"

"Marian Vidal you said? Yes, there usually is some kind of crisis with Mrs. Vidal. Do you know where her room is?"

"Yeah, I know the way."

He walked down the airy corridors, nodding at the more ambulatory residents on his way. He rapped softly on his mother's door.

She wheezed, "Come in."

Pushing the door open, he stepped into the room. She lay propped up on the bed with her oxygen stand next to her, her skin as white as the sheets tucked around her emaciated form.

After assessing her visitor, she closed her eyes. "Oh, it's you."

He stayed by the door and dropped the bag. "Is there some kind of problem? A nurse called me."

Her eyes remained closed. "Why'd she call you? Where's Kate?"

"Kate and Bryan are on vacation in Hawaii with the kids." Some small vestige of compassion made him keep Kate's real mission to himself. Their father hadn't expressed any interest in reconnecting with the wife he abandoned along with his kids, and their mother had no idea her dear departed husband had contacted Kate.

Waving her hand in front of her, she mumbled, "Never had much use for Bryan anyway. And those kids. They run around here screeching and making a ruckus."

He said through clenched teeth, "That's what kids do."

Her eyes flew open. "Did you come here to argue with me? How would you know anyway? You never spend time with your niece and nephews."

"I do when my job allows me to."

She sneered, "Oh, yeah, your precious, secret job."

Crossing his arms to protect himself against all the old hurts, he said, "It pays the bills here."

"Are you going to throw that in my face now? You wouldn't have to be responsible for me if you hadn't driven your own father away." She dissolved into a fit of coughing and hacking.

A muscle twitched in his jaw. "Do you need help?"

She ignored him, and he pressed a button on the wall to summon a nurse.

The nurse bustled into the room and made his mother as comfortable as she could be, and then motioned him out into the hallway.

She asked, "Are you her son?"

"Yes, I'm Justin Vidal."

Shaking her head, she said, "Mr. Vidal, we've caught your mother twice this week sneaking cigarettes."

He shrugged. "What are you going to do? She knows the consequences. She's living the consequences. How's the cirrhosis? Any chance for a transplant?"

The nurse pursed her lips before answering. "The emphysema's too advanced to attempt a transplant. I'm sorry, but I don't think your mother is going to live out the year."

Is that why Kate agreed to this insane meeting with their father? To have a replacement ready? Well, he didn't want a replacement. Didn't need one. His father rejected him once. Why give him another chance? "Is that why you called me?"

A crease lined her brow. "I didn't call you."

"One of the other nurses then? I don't think she gave her name. Just said my mother had some kind of crisis."

The nurse answered, "Could have been, although I wouldn't exactly call this a crisis. I gave your sister this information a few months ago. She didn't tell you?"

He took a deep breath. "I've been working out of the country. So you don't know who called me?"

Glancing at her watch, she shook her head. "I'm sorry, Mr. Vidal, if there's nothing else, I have another patient to see."

He stepped aside to let her pass, returning to his mother's room with his brows drawn together.

His mother rasped out, "What did that nurse have to tell you? Am I dying? It's just as well. I can join your father now. That is if he's dead. I don't even know that. It's your fault he never came back."

She should've thanked him for that, since he'd done what he had back then to protect her. She didn't want his protection then any more than Kate wanted it now. He cut off the familiar refrain. "Do you know who called me to come here?"

Deprived of her favorite subject, she pouted. "I don't know who called you. I don't want you here. Every time I see your face, it reminds me of what you did to your father."

His heart started pumping faster and like a switch, his senses clicked into high gear. The antiseptic smell of the room pricked his nose. The hissing of the oxygen tank blocked out his mother's whining voice. The white walls, floor and bedsheets hurt his eyes.

He bent over and picked up the bag his sister sent over. Dropping it within his mother's reach, he said, "Kate asked me to bring you some things. I have to leave now. Kate will be on vacation for another few weeks, but she'll drop by when she gets back."

He pressed his lips against his mother's dry papery cheek. Her clawlike hands clutched at his arm for a moment.

"Goodbye, Justin."

He escaped from her room. Hearing voices in the front lobby, he slipped out the back door. He began to walk across the parking lot, filling his lungs with fresh air and the sweet fragrance of the flowers that bloomed around the edges of the building.

A voice stopped him.

"Justin!"

Placing a hand on his gun bag, he spun around and looked into the dark eyes of Prasad Mansour.

Chapter Six

Justin pulled out his gun. "Did you set me up?" That's what came of telling people your personal business, letting them into your life…trusting them.

Prasad held his hands out, palms up. "I swear, Justin, I didn't have anything to do with the massacre at the compound."

Holding his weapon steady, Justin asked, "Where were you?"

"I went to Twentynine Palms like I planned. I last saw you at the compound when you and that woman went into the navigation room. I finished taking orders, and I left."

Justin barked, "When did you discover what happened at the compound?"

"When I got back from shopping. I—I saw you, and the woman, at the shopping center in Twentynine Palms. I just figured you finished and were taking her back yourself."

Prasad went on to explain what he found when he got back to the compound—bodies, blood, shell casings.

Hanging his head, he said, "And then I ran."

Justin relaxed his grip on his gun. "Why didn't you call me?"

Prasad hunched his shoulders. "I don't have my agency phone. Didn't have your number. I tracked you to the campsite, but I was afraid to approach you. I thought…"

Justin ground out, "Thought what?"

Looking down, Prasad said, "Thought you might be responsible for that carnage."

His eyes flew to Justin's face. "But I know now. I know you're not a traitor. But neither am I. I'd never betray my country. I'd never betray you."

He wanted to believe him. "You call Leo?"

Prasad nodded. "He won't let me come in. He suspects me just like you do. Won't give me your phone number, either."

Narrowing his eyes, Justin asked, "If Leo suspects you, why doesn't he want you to come in? He suspects me, too, and has been telling me to come in ever since I called him."

Prasad spread his arms out. "I don't know. He…"

Justin gestured behind him at the nursing home. "How'd you know I'd be here? Who set this up?"

Both men jerked their heads in unison toward an oncoming car screeching into the parking lot. The car barreled toward them. Justin pumped off a shot before diving into the bushes that ringed the nursing home.

He heard a thud and a grunt. He twisted his head around. Prasad rolled over the hood of the car. Justin shot into the car once more before crashing through a window of the nursing home.

He hit the floor of the hallway, shards of glass raining down on him. Still gripping his gun, he stood up, crackling bits of window under his feet. Several orderlies and nurses rushed into the hallway.

His mother's nurse cried out, "Mr. Vidal, what's going on?"

He shook his head, sending slivers of glass to the floor, and nodded toward the jagged window. "A car hit someone in the parking lot. He's hurt."

He had to get away. Had to hope Prasad was okay.

Pain cascading down his injured thigh, he jogged down the hallway, ignoring the confusion behind him. He slipped out the front door, gun dangling at his side. Wailing sirens approached. He glanced up and down the street. Curious onlookers, drawn by the sound of tragedy, gathered at office doorways.

Easing into his truck, he waited until the cadre of rescue vehicles passed him, and then he inched down the street, checking all his mirrors. The dark sedan had disappeared. Did his last shot hit the driver?

He drove back to San Diego with one thought circling his brain. If Prasad didn't betray him, who did?

JUSTIN VIDAL WAS a coldhearted bastard.

Lila hacked at her granola with a spoon, breaking it into little bits.

When he talked about his mother in a nursing home, ill, his heartless words fell like flint on her ears. How could he be so cruel?

His eyes. She stopped. His eyes kindled with such emotion. Over the past few days, she'd learned that his amber eyes darkened when he felt something strongly. What was it? Anger? It went beyond anger. Anguish? Whatever it was, she couldn't bear to confront it.

She snorted. Justin Vidal didn't need her to champion him. If his mother's situation tortured him, he sure didn't act like it—whatever those tawny eyes signaled.

Coldhearted bastard.

Cold? She reached up and traced her fingertip along her mouth, still feeling the heat of his lips pressed against hers. When he pulled her close, she felt fire. Hot. And hard.

She jumped up and dumped her half-eaten bowl of granola down the sink. Not her problem anymore. She was out of it.

The phone trilled once. Twice. Mom must still be in the shower.

"Hello?"

"Oh my God, Lila, I'm so glad to hear your voice."

Lila didn't feel that same joy at hearing her neighbor's voice, especially with that tremor around the edges. "Trish? What's wrong?"

Trish took a deep breath. "Two men came to the apartment building looking for you this morning."

Lila's heart flip-flopped. "Two men? Who were they?"

"I don't know. They were foreigners, Indian or Pakistani or something like that. One had an English accent. I told them you were in Mexico. Why aren't you in Mexico?"

Gripping the phone, Lila said, "Slow down, Trish. Did they say who they were?"

She scoffed, "Said they were friends of yours from school. Said you left the dive trip early and they had some of your stuff, but they didn't have any dive gear with them. I didn't believe them for one minute." She paused. "Is it true?"

Lila drew a shaky breath. "It's true I left Mexico early, but I didn't leave anything behind, and I don't know anyone like you described. Except Raj. You know Raj, don't you?"

Trish said, "I know Raj. This wasn't Raj. These guys were scary. Kept darting their eyes around the complex, as if looking for an opportunity to push me inside my apartment and have a go at me."

"Trish, they didn't hurt you?"

"No. You know how we're always complaining about how busy and noisy this place is? Well, today I thanked my lucky stars for it. As usual, there were people all over the place. Then Zig came up. So he immediately got jealous when he saw me talking to these two men. For once, I was grateful for his jealousy, too. He charged up to them bellowing questions, and they took off."

Lila expelled a breath. "So what did you tell them?"

"I told them the truth as far as I knew it. You were still down in Mexico and I hadn't seen you since you left. But even if you were back home, I wouldn't have told them anything. These guys scared me, Lila."

"Did you call the police?"

Trish laughed. "What for, malicious questioning? Lila, what's going on?"

"Nothing. I have no idea why those two men were looking for me, but do me a favor."

"Anything."

"If anyone else comes around asking for me, stay with your original story. I'm still in Mexico. And one more thing."

"What?"

"Have Zig stay with you."

Trish blew out a long breath. "No problem. And Lila?"

"Yeah?"

"You're a terrible liar. Take care of yourself, girl."

Lila replaced the receiver with a shaky hand. They knew who she was. What had Justin said? "They don't know who you are. They're after me anyway."

You're wrong, Justin, she thought.

She glanced around the spacious kitchen, her eyes darting toward the window. How long before they found this place? She'd put the house in Mom's name. It didn't have a mortgage. Monroe was a common name, and the house was far from San Diego County. Could they tie her to Mom, this house?

Should she call Justin? She winced. She didn't even have his number. She didn't even say goodbye. Tears pricked behind her lids.

Staring at the tranquil scene out the window, she massaged her temples. They couldn't track her down here. She kept the apartment in San Diego in her name, so it made sense that they found that location. Legally, this place didn't even belong to her.

She closed her eyes and shook her head as if to clear out the bad thoughts. She'd just have to find another place to live in San Diego. She finished the breakfast dishes and dashed off a note to Mom. Time for a little retail therapy.

She grabbed the keys to Matt's Porsche. He'd left her strict instructions to take his precious car out for a spin or two until he could come home and drive it himself.

Lila browsed the high-end boutiques for a few hours

before sitting down to lunch at an outdoor café. Was it ever going to be safe for her to return to San Diego? What about school? Sounds like they already knew she was a student. And who were "they" anyway? A bunch of nameless, faceless terrorists? How could she ever be safe anywhere?

Her cell phone buzzed in her purse. She checked the display before answering, "Hi, Mom."

Stifling a sob, her mother said, "Lila, you can't come back home."

Fear, like lightning, crackled through her body. "Why not, Mom? What's the matter?"

In a repetition of Trish's words, she said, "Two men came to the house looking for you."

Lila's body sagged, all her breath punched from her lungs. She gasped, "Mom, are you all right? Why are you crying?"

Her mother choked out, "They pushed their way into the house. They threatened me."

Her breath coming in sharp painful gusts, Lila asked, "Did they hurt you?"

"No, I'm just shaken up."

"What did you tell them?"

"I told them you were still in Mexico. That I hadn't heard from you. I don't think they believed me."

Her eyes shifting from table to table on the patio, Lila asked even though she knew the answer, "What did they look like?"

Her mom confirmed her fears. "I think they were Indian. One had a British accent."

Lila checked her watch. The drive from San Diego to Santa Barbara took just over four hours. They must've come here right after leaving Trish. How did they know so much about her, her family? Her heart skittered in her chest. Tyler. Thank God Gareth had him, and he had his father's last name. Her mother had convinced her not to call Tyler yet, since he'd raise a fuss about coming back home. Now she didn't want him home.

Her mom's voice brought her back. "This is connected to that man, isn't it? Justin Vidal."

"Yeah, it is." Lila's brain spun in twenty different directions. Where could she go now? What could she do? She didn't even have Leo's number anymore. Justin took it from her and burned it in the campfire, not wanting her to have any connection to him on her person. The police? Justin told her most law-enforcement agencies weren't even aware of the HIA's existence.

Her mom said, "You have to call him."

Lila sighed. "I can't. I don't know how to reach him."

"I have his cell-phone number. He gave it to me before he left. Told me to give it to you."

"Why didn't you?" So he'd thought of her before he left—a ray of light amid all this darkness.

"I could tell something happened between the two of you the night before he left. You didn't come down to see him off, and he looked so…forbidding. I didn't want to give you the number before you had a chance to cool down, and now I'm glad I waited."

Lila breathed out slowly. "So am I. What's the number?"

Her mother gave her the number, which Lila committed to memory, and told her to be careful. She assured

Lila she'd call the Santa Barbara police. She counted the chief as a special friend of hers, and even if she couldn't tell him why these men were after her daughter, she knew his officers would step up their patrols around the house.

Before she ended the call, her mother voiced Lila's own concerns. "For once, I'm glad Gareth took Tyler away."

"Me, too, Mom."

She paid her bill and retreated to the ladies' room. When it cleared out, she punched in Justin's number on her cell phone.

A voice growled on the other end. "Yeah?"

"Justin?"

He paused. "Who's this?"

"I— It's Lila."

His next question nearly caused her to drop her cell phone in the toilet. "What kind of sandwiches did we buy in the desert, and what did I remove from mine?"

Her mind clicked back to the convenience store, and she answered, "Turkey, avocado and sprouts. You picked off the sprouts."

He expelled his breath. "What's wrong?"

"They found me."

His voice vibrated across the phone. "Are you all right?"

Propping herself up against the stall door, she answered, "I'm okay. I wasn't home…at either place."

"At either place? What do you mean?"

She swallowed before continuing. "My friend in San Diego called me. She said two guys came looking for me at our apartment complex. Then while I was shopping downtown, my mom called me. The same two men came to the house in Santa Barbara."

"Is she okay?"

"She's fine and calling in reinforcements from the police chief."

He asked, his voice tight, "Where are you now?"

She gave a shaky laugh. "I'm in a bathroom stall in a restaurant in downtown Santa Barbara."

"Can you get down here to San Diego? I'm not at the place in University City anymore. I relocated to a house in Encinitas. A safe house. Although I don't know how much safer you'll be with me, but at least you won't be on your own."

I'll always be safe with you… She said, "Did something happen? Did they find you, too?"

He told her about the ambush at the nursing home and about Prasad. "Ironically, I think the only one I can trust now is Prasad, and he's lying in a hospital bed with a concussion."

And he trusted her. She had to help him, show him that he hadn't misplaced his trust.

He repeated, "Can you get down here?"

"Yeah, I have a car, and I can stop at the bank for some money."

"Don't bother with that right now. Get out of Santa Barbara as fast as you can. I'll expect you some time tonight. If anything happens on the drive down, you suspect someone's following you, anything, drive straight to a police station or highway-patrol office. Give them this name and phone number."

He gave her the name and number of a San Diego

sheriff's deputy, Fletcher Bale, and then he gave her directions to his own location in Encinitas.

"Lila?"

The sound of her name on his lips felt like a caress, and she shivered. "Yes?"

"Be careful."

HE SLAMMED the cell phone into the palm of his hand. How had they found her? They weren't followed. He'd never revealed her last name to anyone. They never even got a good look at her, except the agents at the compound. And they were all dead.

His breath hissed through his teeth. Fingerprints. They took her fingerprints from the compound—the wand, the doorjamb, the screen itself. From there they'd traced her easily. She'd admitted herself she had a police record.

He glanced at his watch. Three o'clock. It took all his self-control not to jump in his truck and drive up to Santa Barbara to get her. She had to be safe. He had to see her again.

Instead he called Fletcher Bale.

"Bale here."

"It's Vidal. Were you able to do what I asked?"

"Just a minute."

A car door slammed before Fletch got back on the line. "Prasad Mansour died in the parking lot of the Oasis Valley Nursing Home, the victim of a hit-and-run driver. Harish Vanju is now safe in the Carlsbad Hospital with a security guard stationed at his door."

Justin heaved a sigh. "Thanks, man. Is he still unconscious?"

"Yeah, still unconscious, but the doctors are hopeful.

We called in his parents like you suggested. The doctor thinks it's a good idea, too."

"Were you able to handle the Carlsbad Police Department, Fletch?"

"Your name's been completely expunged from all records. Harish sustained his injuries in a one-car accident on the I-5."

"I owe you, Fletch."

"Big-time."

He'd wrongly accused Prasad. He wasn't the traitor. When he confronted him in the parking lot, the kid was scared out of his mind. Why didn't Leo bring him in if he suspected him?

Justin had been ignoring Leo's frequent calls. He picked up once or twice just to tell Leo he was okay and still planning to go to Mexico. Leo didn't know anything about the tunnel either. Besides Chad and himself, only Danny Molina knew about the tunnel. Where was Molina?

When Chad called him from Mexico City, he said Molina had gone off to Costa Rica on a lead. Said he was glad to be rid of him. Why hadn't Molina called in yet? Leo hadn't heard from him, either.

He rubbed his hands across his face. Lila would be here in another three hours. He should get some food in for tonight and tomorrow morning. And after that? He may just have to take her to Mexico with him. It would be easier for him to find that clearing with her guidance. His gut clenched at the thought of dragging her back into danger, but now it looked as if he wouldn't have to do any dragging.

Danger already knew her name.

FOUR HOURS LATER, Justin paced a groove in the hardwood floor of the sparsely furnished living room. He rushed to the window every time a car drove down the street.

Finally, he saw an expensive sports car crawl past the house and then back up. Lila. He waited on the porch while she slid one lovely leg out the door, her head of tousled, gleaming curls dipping as she ducked out of the small car. She floated toward him, a small purse dangling from her shoulder.

Springing down the steps, he said, "I thought you'd never get here."

He took her hand, pulling her into the house. When he shut the door behind them, he gathered her in his arms, wrapping around her as if this could keep her out of harm's way. If only he had a magic ritual to make it that simple.

Her heart skipped against his chest. A small tremble rippled through her body, and he squeezed tighter.

Placing his hands on her shoulders, he nudged her away to look into her eyes. "You worried the hell out of me. What took you so long?"

She gave a shuddering breath. "I stopped a few times. Got some money from the bank." She held up a small bag. "Picked up a toothbrush and a few other things. I left the house for a shopping trip, not a jaunt to another country."

Yeah, he'd have a hard time leaving her here even if he wanted to. He raised his brows. "Who said anything about a jaunt to another country?"

She shrugged bare shoulders under his clasp. "We're going to Mexico, aren't we? We won't be safe until we find that tunnel again and destroy it."

He released her. "You catch on quickly."

Dropping her bag on the lone couch in the room, she said, "Can I have one of those cool code names now?"

He stepped back. "You're not scared?" He'd expected tears and hysterics when she showed up. Instead she cracked jokes and looked as cool as a long drink of water.

She sank down on the couch. "Terrified. What better time to joke? My dad taught me that."

She pointed to his leg. "How's the bullet wound? Still taking your antibiotics?"

"It's fine. Your mom did a great job."

Leaning back against a cushion, she asked, "So how'd they find me?"

He rubbed his face. "Fingerprints I think."

She sat upright. "From the HIA compound?"

He nodded. Definitely a quick study.

"If not Prasad, then who's the traitor?"

Shrugging, he said, "It could be anybody."

He didn't want to think about which of his coworkers turned against his country, against him. He pushed the thought to the back of his mind.

He said, "I think I have some information on the guy in the trunk of Chad's car."

She gasped. "Did you find him?"

He hated giving her any more bad news, but she had a right to know. "Someone found him, all right...dead."

She hugged herself while he explained about the dead body in the same general area of his house. "They must've dragged him out of that trunk right after you parked the car and dumped his body. Probably just wanted to make sure he was dead and wouldn't be telling any tales."

Shaking her head, she said, "I still don't understand

how they managed to put a man in the trunk of the car without waking me."

"That's something else I discovered. Do you remember drinking from a bottle of water that night?"

She nodded, eyes wide.

"Have you ever heard of valerian root?"

"No."

He explained, "It's an herb, a natural sleeping pill. Chad mixed some pills extracted from valerian root into the bottle of water. I discovered it in his car."

Running her hands through her hair, she said, "That explains a lot. So he wasn't as careless as you first thought. At least he intended that I sleep through his entire meeting with the coyote just in case something went wrong."

His lips formed a grim line. Then he said, "That doesn't excuse him. He should've never dragged you into this." He stopped. Wasn't he just as guilty?

Gesturing into the kitchen, he said, "I'll make some dinner. Are you hungry?"

She laughed. "Now I'm really terrified. You cook?"

"Necessity. I've pretty much always lived alone. There's a barbecue on the deck out back. I marinated a couple of steaks… I can throw them on the grill when you're ready."

He stopped and turned on his way to the kitchen. "You're not a vegetarian or anything like that are you?"

She assured him, "Nothing like that."

He grabbed some matches from a drawer and went outside to light the barbecue.

Her voice wafted out to the deck. "What is this place? Is it yours?"

The flames raced along the charcoal, and he walked

back inside. Her presence infused the plain room with vibrancy and color. The blues and greens of her sundress swirled around her long tanned legs, making her look like an exotic flower growing in the middle of the floor. "Actually it belongs to Sam Clemens."

Wrinkling her nose, she asked, "Who's Sam Clemens? Friend of yours?"

"A very good friend. Meet Sam Clemens." He spread his arms wide.

Her brows shot up. "You're Sam Clemens? Is that your cover?"

"That's the name I used to buy this place anyway. The other place near University City is a rental under the name of Tom Finn."

She laughed. "Sam Clemens, Tom Sawyer, Huckleberry Finn. I see a pattern here. Do you like Mark Twain by any chance?"

"He's my favorite writer."

She mused, "He was a sad man despite the humor in his books."

That clear blue gaze penetrated his soul, and he dipped his head to escape it. "I know."

He headed back to the kitchen, calling over his shoulder, "Would you like some red wine? I already made the salad, and I'll put the steaks on in another minute."

She agreed to the wine, following him into the kitchen. She pulled some dishes from the cupboard and laid out the plates on a little table on the deck.

She asked, "Is it okay if I pick some of those flowers in the front?"

He had flowers in the front? He answered, "Sure."

She returned with a bunch of purple flowers and

found a vase in the cupboard. She arranged the flowers and placed the vase in the center of the table.

When he finished grilling the steaks, they sat across from each other, knees meeting under the table.

He touched his wineglass to hers. "Here's to finding that tunnel and getting your son and your life back."

Looking at him over the rim of the wineglass, she asked, "And what about for you?"

He sipped his wine. "I want to find that tunnel, and I want to find out who betrayed me…his country."

"What else do you want, Justin Vidal?"

You. In my arms. In my bed. He shook his head. "The tunnel. That's enough for now."

As they dug into their food, he changed the subject. He could be on 24/7, but he didn't expect her to be. Eventually, the conversation led to her son.

"I just want to be a good mom. I hate all the drama with Gareth."

She played with the remaining steak on her plate, and without looking up asked, "How'd it go with your mother? Was the whole thing a setup? She wasn't ill after all?"

He expected this. He both welcomed and dreaded it.

Ever since that moment he saw the distaste in her eyes when he'd talked of his mother, he wanted to erase it. Replace it with…what? Not pity. He hated pity.

"Despite the setup, my mother is very ill. She has cirrhosis of the liver and emphysema. Years of drinking and smoking."

"Oh, I see."

He raised his brows. "And what do you see?"

Tracing a pattern with her knife on the plate, she

answered, "It's hard to muster much sympathy for someone with those diseases. They bring them on through their own bad habits, but they're just bad habits, not inherent evils."

He rubbed his forehead. "It's more than that, Lila. My mother finds my company distasteful because my father left the family, and she blames me for it. Always has."

"Why?"

"Because it's true."

"How old were you when he left?"

"Fifteen."

She gasped. "Your mother blames a fifteen-year-old boy? That's absurd."

He drew a long breath, gulped his wine and poured some more. "Not really."

"What did you do at fifteen to drive your father away?"

He set down his wineglass. "I beat him to a bloody pulp. He left that night and never came back."

Her hand flew to her mouth. She whispered, "Why?"

He closed his eyes. Images of his miserable childhood marched across his mind—the alcohol-fueled violence, the fights, the need to protect his mother and sister. "My father was an abusive alcoholic, but my mother wouldn't leave him. As I got older and stronger, I tried a few times to protect my mother against him, but she wouldn't have it."

In fact, she told him to stop interfering in her life. Her life! As if the fights and abuse didn't affect him and Kate.

"Then one night…" He gripped the stem of the wineglass so tightly, he almost snapped it.

Her eyes wide, she asked, "What happened?"

"He went after Kate, my sister."

"He tried to beat her up?"

He clenched his jaw before answering. "Worse. He went into her bedroom. She cried out, and I rushed into her room."

"How old was Kate?"

"She was fifteen. We're twins. When I saw him in her room, on her bed, I went crazy. I beat him with my fists until he was a puddle on the floor. Nobody called the police. What explanation could they give? He slinked out of the house that night, and we never saw him again."

She shook her head. "Your mother should've been glad to see him go."

He'd never forget the fury his mother turned on him when she realized her miserable husband wasn't coming back. When he drove his father off, he expected some acknowledgement from his mother, some admission the she'd made a mistake staying with that man. Raising his shoulders, he said, "Should've been but wasn't. Let's just say our standard of living declined sharply after he left."

"That's all she cared about? She didn't care about her daughter? Her son?" Her voice caught.

She pushed back from the little table and came around behind his chair. Placing her hands on the sides of his neck, she traced her thumbs along his jaw.

Tipping his head back, he closed his eyes. She leaned over him, her silky curls falling over his face. He inhaled her feminine scent, more intoxicating than the fruity red wine.

She sealed her mouth over his, and he sucked in

her lower lip, nibbling on its sweetness. Her soft breasts crushed against him, and he reached up to stroke their fullness.

She whispered against his lips, "I'm sorry."

He dropped his hands. Jumping up from the table, he banged her chin with the top of his head.

He rasped out, "My God, I don't need your pity. I don't need anyone. It's why they call me Lone Wolf."

Chapter Seven

Lila bit her tongue. A sharp pain stung her chin.

Justin loomed in front of her, his chest rising and falling with each heavy breath. From the passion they'd just shared? Or from his anger?

Rubbing her jaw, she demanded, "What are you talking about?"

When they kissed and his lips moved against hers and his hands cupped her breasts, she hadn't been thinking about charity. She hadn't been thinking at all. She'd just wanted back in his arms. Still wanted that, but the wall he'd just constructed may as well have been built of brick instead of hurt and misunderstanding.

He glared down at her from a hundred miles away. "I'm not one of your…lost causes."

She sputtered, "Who said you were? I don't kiss lost causes. I meant, I was sorry I misjudged you before you went to see your mother."

He sliced his hand through the air and then turned his back on her. He grabbed and stacked the plates, almost cracking them.

She blinked, opened her mouth and stopped. Obviously he didn't care to hear her explanation. The impenetrability of his armor depended on believing his own tapes running through his head, not his own feelings. God, she had to resort to psychobabble to understand this man. Why bother?

Even if her blood still simmered from his touch.

Carrying the dishes into the kitchen, he brushed past her. She drew back. Better to keep her distance, emotionally and physically. His very nearness prompted her nerve endings to dance in response and anticipation. And he wasn't about to deliver.

The dishes clattered into the sink. A glass broke.

She drew up next to him, hands clasped behind her back. "Can I help?"

He turned to her with two large pieces of glass in his hands. Did that dark shadow on his face signal regret? For his flare-up, or for the glass?

Shrugging, he said, "It's okay. I'll wrap these up and toss them in the trash."

When he moved away from the sink, she took his place and began washing the dishes while he cleared up the remnants of the dinner they'd shared outside. They carefully skirted each other in the small kitchen.

She broke the silence. "Are we going to Mexico tomorrow?"

He spoke over his shoulder, "Probably the next day. There are a few things I want to check on first."

Turning and gesturing to her sundress, he said, "You should buy some more appropriate clothes for a road trip. I'll leave you some money."

"I have money."

"Oh, yeah, I forgot. You're rich."

She winced. She wanted to bring him back to that place they'd inhabited during dinner. That place that soothed him, made him want to open up to her. Her ill-chosen words had made him snap shut. Who knew such a tough guy could be so touchy?

Sitting down at his laptop, he said, "This place has only one bathroom. Go ahead and shower first. There's a clean towel on the rack, and I left you one of my T-shirts. You can have my bedroom. The other room doesn't have a bed."

She started to protest, but he cut her off by raising his hands. Scooping up her bag, she retreated to the bathroom.

THE WARM WATER funneled over her body, and she lifted her face to the stream. The water carried her tears down the drain.

Did he willfully choose to misunderstand her? Or was he just so prickly he couldn't help himself?

Maybe she should just go away. Those men already checked her apartment. Perhaps she could just go back there. Finish her research, pick up Ty and return to Santa Barbara before classes started again. The bad guys would probably be too busy chasing after Justin in Mexico to bother about her anymore.

But the thought of exposing Ty to any danger sent waves of nausea to the pit of her stomach. She'd have to see this through. Then she'd forget all about Lone Wolf. Forget the way his tawny eyes kindled with passion. Forget the smooth, firm texture of his skin. Forget the caress of his lips.

She groaned and welcomed the pounding spray on her upturned face.

After drying off, she wrapped the towel around her body and slipped into the one completely furnished room in the stark house. The large tall post mahogany bed matched the heavy dresser and two nightstands. An intricately carved bookshelf, crammed with books, commanded one corner of the room. She studied its contents—history, politics, biography, and, she smiled, spy novels.

She dropped the towel over the back of a chair and scooped up the T-shirt he'd left her. She pulled it over her head, disappointed by the smell of detergent—nothing left of him. She slid between the sheets of the large bed. They smelled freshly laundered, but she knew he'd slept on them the night before. The clean scent of soap and the muskiness of his masculinity lingered in their folds. She rolled onto her stomach and buried her face in his pillow, breathing deeply.

A rap on the door spun her around. She sat up against the pillows, clutching the sheet to her chest, and called out, "Yes?"

He answered from outside the door, "Can I talk to you a minute?"

"Yes." She gripped the sheet tighter. Would he apologize? Take up where they left off on the patio? Her bare skin tingled with the possibilities, her nipples leading the way.

He opened the door and stepped into the room. A shard of moonlight beamed a path in front of him, but he avoided it, remaining in the darkness. "I just talked to a friend of mine. Prasad regained consciousness."

She nodded. Business, not pleasure.

Brushing his hair back from his face, he said, "I want to see him before we go to Mexico."

She longed to replace his hands with her own. "Should I go with you?"

He blew out a breath. "Yeah, I think that's best. Get some sleep for now."

She nodded as he left her there...alone. *Sleep? With you in the next room?*

The clatter of the keyboard echoed through the empty house. Empty except for this room. His refuge? Why was he so afraid to put down roots? To belong to someplace permanent? Someone. Twenty years is a long time to carry that kind of loneliness inside. She sighed and changed position, again.

She heard the front door open, and she sat upright. Voices carried through the closed door and into the bedroom. Had those two men finally found her? She bounded out of bed, yanked off her T-shirt and grabbed her sundress. Pulling it over her head, she stumbled to the door. She eased it open, putting her eye to the crack.

A woman. A woman in Justin's arms.

She pulled open the door and tripped into the living room as if she had every right. "What's going on?"

The petite brunette lifted a tear-streaked face from Justin's shoulder. "Oh, I—I'm sorry, Justin."

He settled the woman on the couch and sank down next to her. "It's okay, Brooke. This is Lila."

Lila's eyes drilled into the woman seated on the couch next to Justin, one small hand clasped between his two strong ones. Did he prefer helpless women?

He turned to Brooke. "Do you want a glass of wine?"

Lila clenched her jaw. Their wine. The wine they never got to finish.

Brooke nodded, her straight silky hair falling over her shoulders.

"Lila, would you please get Brooke some wine?" He added, "Get the box of tissues from the bathroom, too."

A frown tugged at the corners of Lila's lips as she poured a glass of wine and grabbed the tissues. She rushed back to the living room, absurdly not wanting to leave the two of them alone.

Justin focused his attention on Brooke. "Tell me what happened."

Brooke drew a shaky breath, thanked Lila for the wine and tissues and took a swig from the glass. "It's Danny."

He said, "I figured as much. Go on."

Brooke blew her nose. "He called me from Costa Rica. He's in trouble, Justin."

Lila released her cooped-up breath, her natural empathy coursing through her veins again. This must be another agent's wife or girlfriend.

Justin frowned. "What kind of trouble?"

She continued, "One of his sources called him from Costa Rica with a tip. That's why he left Mexico City. But when he got to their meeting place, his source never showed up. Then someone shot at him."

He asked, "Was he hit?"

Rubbing her arms, she said, "No. He managed to hide out with his contact's family for a while. The wife hadn't seen her husband in two days. Not since he called Danny."

"Did Danny call in?"

She shook her head. "No, something his source said makes him think whoever's behind everything is someone on the inside." She avoided his eyes.

He pinned hers. "Does he suspect me?"

She spread out her arms. "He suspects everyone right now."

Justin murmured, "I know the feeling."

She cried, "You have to help him, Justin. There's no one else."

He crossed his arms. "He didn't send you to find me."

Flinging out her hands, she said, "He's not thinking clearly, but the way he talks about you... Hell, you're the only one at the HIA he socializes with. I know once he thinks it over, he'll contact you."

Justin breathed out. Before he could say anything, Brooke continued, "He blamed Chad at first. He complained he never took him into his confidence. Had the feeling he knew something he wasn't telling, so maybe you could start with Chad."

"Chad's dead."

Her shoulders heaved, and she pressed a fist to her mouth.

Justin mechanically handed her another tissue. "You said 'at first' he suspected Chad. What then?"

She sniffled. "The informant indicated someone higher up was calling the shots...literally in his case."

He said sharply, "Leo?"

"I don't know. He didn't mention any names. It's all speculation anyway. He never got to meet with his source. Can you help him?"

"Does he want my help?"

She jumped up from the couch. "He wants to find what Chad was looking for. The same thing that obviously got Chad killed. I just want him home."

He stood up next to her. "I don't have the power to bring him home if he doesn't want to come home."

Her face contorted. "Damn you. And damn him, too. I'm sick of it all. First he skipped off to Afghanistan, then Jakarta, now Mexico. Are you just going to chase these people all over the world until…until what?" She collapsed on the couch, crying into her hands.

Lila sat down next to her, putting her arm around her.

Brooke jerked away. "Are you one of them?"

Lila assured her she wasn't while Justin paced the room.

He stopped in front of them. "The next time you talk to Danny, tell him Chad's dead and I'm on my way to Mexico. Tell him to meet me in a little town called Loma Vista, just inland from the coast and about an hour south of the border."

He continued, "Don't talk to anyone about Danny. All you know is that he's in Mexico."

She twisted her lips. "Don't worry. Nobody from the HIA even knows I exist. We live in a house owned by Stephen Crane."

Lila stifled a laugh, and Justin quirked an eyebrow at her. "He stole that idea from me."

Brooke asked, "What are you going to do?"

He rubbed his chin. "I'm going to pay a visit to the HIA field office in San Diego."

When Justin left the house to make sure the coast was clear, Brooke turned to Lila and said, "Don't do it."

Lila drew back. "Do what?"

Gesturing to Justin outside, she said, "Get involved with him. You'll never know a moment's peace."

"Why do you stay with Danny?"

Brooke's eyes opened wide. "I love him."

THE NEXT MORNING Lila stood in front of Justin, hands on her hips, eyes wide. "We're going shopping? Our lives hang in the balance, and you want to check out the sales?"

"That's our cover. The HIA field office is across the street from an outdoor mall." His eyes traveled the length of her body and back up again. "Besides, I'm sick of seeing you in the same clothes all the time."

Her palpitating heart owed as much to that tawny gaze flickering over her body, as to the realization that he wasn't angry anymore. Or at least he'd shelved it for now.

A smile touched her lips. "I can definitely pretend to shop, but can I also help with the stakeout? I'll do whatever you tell me to do. I'll even carry that gun again."

His jaw dropped. "God help us. The best way you can assist with the surveillance is to play your part and keep out of sight. Get your purse and hang this camera on your shoulder. We're tourists…on a shopping spree."

He slung a pair of binoculars around his neck and pulled a baseball cap low over his eyes, tucking his hair up in the back.

Eyeing her low-heeled, strappy sandals, he asked, "Do you have another pair of shoes?"

She glanced down at her feet. "No, typically I don't pack an extra pair of shoes when I go shopping in downtown Santa Barbara. Why? You think we'll have to make a run for it?"

He clicked his gun bag around his hips. "You never know."

The HIA field office hid in plain sight among the glittering high-rises of a revitalized downtown. Lila swallowed hard. Gareth's company, TouchStone, commanded several floors in the tallest tower.

She closed her eyes as a longing for Tyler flowed through her veins.

She wandered in and out of the stores clustered in an outdoor mall across the street from the building that housed the anonymous HIA field office. Justin, her indulgent husband, trailed behind her, anxious to return to his sightseeing.

He parked himself in front of one boutique's window with a view of the street.

Lila paraded out of the dressing room in a pair of tiny shorts cut too low to be decent and a midriff top.

"How about this, honey?" Revenge for breaking away from the most delicious kiss she'd had in a long time. The most delicious kiss since the previous one he broke away from.

His eyes lit up and he swallowed—hard, before he intoned, "A little inappropriate."

Laughing, she returned to the dressing room, feeling his eyes glued to her swaying backside.

She changed back into her sundress and wondered how much longer he planned to watch the building. He hadn't discovered anything yet, and he wouldn't go into the office itself. She walked out of the dressing room and stopped.

"Justin?"

He was hunched over in a corner of the shop behind a mannequin in a miniskirt, his hands cupped around his face, pressed against the window.

"Sir?" Leaning over the counter, the sales assistant drew her brows together.

Justin jumped back, nearly taking out the mannequin, and grabbed Lila's arm. "Let's go."

"Th-the shorts?" The sales assistant scurried from behind the counter, and Lila tossed the shorts to her as Justin yanked her out the door.

He dropped onto a bench, pulling her down with him, and trained his binoculars on the plaza of the building across the street.

"What are you looking at?"

"Woman by the fountain, talking on a cell phone. Recognize her?"

Lila squinted into the glare, scanning the fountain. Her eyes shifted to a tall, dark-haired woman on the phone. She didn't recognize her from this distance.

Justin handed her the binoculars and bent over to rustle in one of the bags.

Lila tracked the woman, brought her into focus and gasped. "It can't be. She's dead."

He ground out, "Looks like Victoria Lang is alive and well. And we're going to pay her a congratulatory visit. Correction. I'm going to pay her that visit. Wait here."

He loped across the street and came up on the other side of the fountain, approaching Victoria from behind.

She spit her words into the phone, gesticulating with one hand. "We have enough. I don't like it."

Waiting until she ended the call, he sidled up next to her and pressed his gun against her ribs.

He growled in her ear, "So you made a miraculous escape from the compound."

Stiffening, she answered, "Justin, thank God you're okay. We've been trying to get you to come in."

He said between clenched teeth, "I know you have. I just don't know for what purpose."

She turned her head, flashing a smile. "Let's sit down and talk. You don't need the gun."

"It makes me feel whole." He propelled her toward a bench facing the building and at right angles to the sidewalk.

She lowered her tall frame to the bench, crossing long slim legs and said, "We think the person behind everything is Prasad."

Ignoring the accusation for now, he said, "How'd you get away?"

She glanced up at the building. "I wasn't there. I was planning on going to Vegas for some R & R the next morning. Remember? After Prasad left for rations, I decided to make an early start."

He remembered she'd had a bag over her shoulder. What did she have in that bag? "How convenient. Hope your luck continued to hold out in Vegas."

Licking her lips, she shifted away from his gun. "I didn't even go back to the compound. Leo called and told me what happened. Said he suspected Prasad... or you."

"Funny, Leo never mentioned your narrow escape to me."

"How could he? You won't give him two minutes on the phone."

"I have my own agenda right now."

Shaking her head, she said, "You always do."

She continued to cast furtive looks up at the building,

so he kept his eyes focused on the front doors. Was she signaling someone?

He asked, "Why do you think it's Prasad?"

She widened artfully lined eyes. "He tried to kill you at the nursing home."

"He didn't try to kill me. How do you know about that meeting anyway?"

Smoothing the silk of her skirt, she said, "We set it up. We wanted to bring in both you and Prasad to sort this all out. We're all in danger. Our ops in the parking lot said Prasad drew his gun on you."

"You better find new ops. Is that why they charged both of us with the car?"

She explained, "They didn't have a chance to do anything else. It worked, didn't it? They hit Prasad. He's dead."

"Your ops do sloppy work."

She put her hand on his arm, her long nails digging into his skin. He flinched. "They're your ops, too, Justin. It's safe to come in. Leo's in the office right now. Come on up and bring the witness with you."

His hand tightened on his weapon. "She's not with me anymore."

Her green eyes flickered. "Was she able to tell you anything? The place where Chad died?"

A horn blared. Brakes squealed. His name rose above the cacophony. "Justin!"

He swiveled his head to the right and saw Lila dodging traffic, her shopping bags swinging from her arms, the binoculars banging against her chest.

Lila screamed, "The fountain, the fountain!"

He ducked down before he turned to look toward the

fountain. A man, his hand shoved in the pocket of his jacket, crouched behind the stone dolphin frolicking in the spray of water.

Justin rolled sideways as a bullet smacked the back of the bench. Victoria lunged the other way, staggering to her feet.

Lila reached the curb, but Justin spun her around. He plunged into the traffic, dragging her with him with one arm, his gun still clutched in the other. They dodged between cars as the drivers honked and yelled obscenities.

Glancing back, he saw the gunman turn from the street and raise his weapon at Victoria's retreating back. He didn't stick around to see if the shooter hit his mark.

People screamed and stampeded out of the plaza, further snarling traffic.

He grabbed Lila's clammy hand and jerked her through the streets back to the alley where they'd parked the truck. He shoved her into the truck and entered on the other side.

Rolling out of the alley, he looked over at her. She stared straight ahead gulping air, those shopping bags still twined around her arms.

Reaching over and tracing a scratch along her cheek, he said, "You want one of those cool code names now?"

Chapter Eight

She wasn't sleeping in his T-shirt anymore. She bought a nightgown yesterday, a floating cloud of sheer silk. He didn't know which was worse, imagining her bare skin against his sheets, or imagining her nude body draped in that piece of white confection.

He glanced at his bedroom door, still closed despite the rustling and clinking of his morning routine. She deserved to sleep late after yesterday's adventure. She saved him. He was so intent on the entrance to the building, he failed to notice the man stealing across the plaza toward Victoria and him. But Lila noticed him. Saw him through the binoculars. Maybe she'd failed her father once, but she was batting a thousand for him.

He sat down at the laptop, a cup of coffee warming his hands. Every day he spent with her she punched holes in his expectations. It would've been so much easier if he could have dismissed her as an airhead.

He experienced sheer hell sleeping on the couch these past two nights while she snuggled in his bed. Sheer. Was that nightgown an invitation? She chose it over much more serviceable garments, even watched his face while she picked it out, running her delicate fingers through its silky folds.

Was she telling him the truth the other night? He didn't exactly see pity in her face when he spun his sad tale. Anger maybe. Indignation definitely.

That wasn't pity in her touch or her kiss, either. Remembering her warm, wet mouth, a charge jolted through his body and his groin tightened. She'd felt good against him, soft, sweet. He could've feasted on her honeyed lips all night.

But he could only hear, "I'm sorry." He didn't want her to feel sorry for him. Didn't want her on those terms. Easy terms. She cared for everyone the same way. Chad, her brother, maybe that ex-husband of hers...once. Were they all stand-ins for the father she couldn't save with her love?

He shook his head. Not important now.

He tried calling Victoria last night on her agency phone, but she wasn't answering. Because she didn't want to explain what happened out there in front of the HIA field office, or because she was dead? A blurb on the news reported a shooting in the plaza, but made no mention of any injuries. He came up short with Fletch, too. No reports of dead bodies turning up anywhere near the downtown area.

He didn't tell Fletch the possible body belonged to Victoria.

The bedroom door eased open and Lila poked her head out. "Am I too late to come with you to see Prasad?"

He returned, "I wouldn't leave home without you. You're my lucky charm."

She flashed a smile and, holding her small bag in

front of her, clothes draped across her arm, scurried to the bathroom.

Catching just a flash of thigh under the swinging silk, he gulped his coffee and burned his throat. "Damn."

Two hours later, the antiseptic hospital smell burned his nose. Fletch waited for them in the hallway outside Prasad's private room. His presence surprised Justin. Obviously he took his resettling efforts on Prasad's behalf very seriously.

As he extended his hand to Justin, he said, "Did you talk to Dr. Levine yet?"

"Yeah, doesn't want him too excited. Fletch, this is Lila Monroe. Lila, this is Fletcher Bale, a former HIA drone."

Fletch shook Lila's hand. "Seems to me you're forgetting the 'former' part lately."

"We could really use you back, Fletch. Now more than ever."

Fletch grimaced. "So I gather. I'm going to take off and leave you to your reunion."

Prasad jerked his head up when Justin and Lila entered his room, and winced.

Justin grinned. "Careful throwing that head around. You don't want to break it again."

Prasad beamed. "No thanks to you."

"Hey, you could've jumped through the window with me."

Prasad plucked at his sheets. "Thanks, man, for arranging this and for believing me."

Justin's voice roughened. "Save your thanks. I tried and convicted you, but I hoped like hell I was wrong.

Hey, I trained you, didn't I? How'd you track us to Cottonwood anyway?"

"It's like you said. You trained me. I saw you take the turn toward Joshua Tree National Park and figured you had to be in one of the three campsites there."

Justin gestured to Lila hanging back by the door. "Do you remember Lila?"

Prasad waved. "How could I forget? All the trouble started with her."

Looking back at Lila, Justin chuckled. "Yeah, it did, didn't it." More trouble than Prasad could ever know.

Justin updated Prasad on Danny Molina and told him about seeing Victoria yesterday.

Prasad's mouth hung open. "Do you think she and Leo are in on this thing together?"

This was the second time someone had mentioned Leo, first Brooke and now Prasad. "I'm not sure. What makes you think Leo is the traitor?"

Prasad scratched at the bandage on his head. "You know why Victoria's marriage broke up, don't you?"

"You mean, besides the regular stress and strain of this job?"

"She was having an affair…with Leo."

Justin's eyes narrowed. "How do you know this?"

"I saw them together once in Vegas. She always took R & R there from the compound in Twentynine Palms. One time I decided to join her there, but I never got the chance. I saw her in the casino with Leo. They were totally engrossed in each other and didn't even notice me."

Leo and Victoria? Man, was he out of the loop. "Did you ever ask her about it?"

"No. I didn't want to embarrass her. She was still

married at the time, and Leo's still married. Don't you think that's important now in light of Victoria's behavior yesterday? Gives her a motive for working with Leo."

"If she's still alive."

Lila spoke up for the first time. "I just don't get why the terrorists are chasing us all over the place. Why don't they just go down to Mexico and start using that tunnel?"

Justin chewed on the side of his thumb. "Maybe the guys down there don't know where it is."

She threw out her hands. "But they were right there. Chad said, 'The tunnel is here.' Even if the men couldn't understand his Spanish, they just had to conduct a search of the immediate area. How hard could it be to find the entrance to the tunnel once they knew the location?"

He'd worried this idea before like a loose tooth. Why were they bothering with them if they knew the tunnel's location? If. Maybe they didn't know. Maybe Chad meant to throw them off with that statement, and the tunnel wasn't there at all. Maybe just the two killers knew the location of the meeting place and took that knowledge with them to the grave.

"Lila, what happened after they shot Chad and you took off? Did the Mexicans kill the men who shot Chad?"

Catching her lower lip in her teeth, she shook her head. "I don't know what happened. I was scared, confused. I just wanted to get out of there."

A cold puff of fear touched the back of his neck, making the hair there quiver. If Al Tariq still didn't know where that tunnel was, they'd want Lila to show them. "Maybe the men who shot Chad never had a chance to pass along the information about the tunnel. Maybe Al Tariq doesn't know where it is."

Prasad suggested, "What about the Border Patrol? Can we send them down there to look for the tunnel?"

"Not without any proof or a definite location. I'm taking Lila with me. She's going to try to find it again."

Prasad sat up straighter. "I'm going with you."

Justin countered, "Oh no you're not. Not with that bandage plastered on your head."

Prasad ripped the bandage from his forehead, revealing fresh stitches. "I'm going."

A man and a woman entered the room with books, magazines and food.

Justin asked, "Are these your parents?"

Prasad murmured, "Yeah."

"Good, then maybe they can talk some sense into that broken skull of yours."

Prasad made the introductions, and Mr. Mansour pumped Justin's hand. "Thank you for saving my son's life."

Justin cocked his head. "Are you sure you got the story right? I'm the one who left him in the parking lot for dead."

The older man swept his arm in the air. "I don't mean that. Because of your training, he was able to save himself. He doesn't tell me much about what he does, but he told me that."

Prasad's mother, her dark eyes shimmering, nodded and reached up to place a kiss on Justin's cheek. A warm flush crept up from his neck to his forehead.

Prasad laughed. "You see what I'm up against?"

Justin swallowed. "You're very lucky." He turned to Prasad's parents. "Now, tell him he's not going anywhere until the doctor gives him the all clear."

They assured him they'd keep an eye on their son, and Justin and Lila left the hospital not much wiser.

Standing by Justin's truck, Lila asked, "Now what? Are you going to contact Leo?"

He plucked his cell phone out of his pocket. "I've been trying. All of a sudden he's not so interested in talking to me."

He punched in Leo's number again and shook his head at Lila. "He's not answering."

She put her hand on his arm. "Can we have lunch? I'm starving."

Her touch acted like a tranquilizer, smoothing out the worry and rough edges. For the first time that day, he noticed the warmth of the sun tempered by the cool, salty ocean breeze.

He squeezed her hand. "So am I."

They stopped at a beachside café, bright and cheery with red-and-white-striped umbrellas.

After they ordered burgers and iced teas, Lila looked into his eyes. "I don't pity you. I totally understand your feelings about your parents."

He drew in a deep breath. "I don't think you do."

Holding up her hands, she said, "Okay, I know you don't want understanding, either."

"It's getting complicated, Lila. Our father contacted my sister."

She raised her eyebrows. "He's still alive?"

"Unfortunately. He contacted her several months ago. He's sober and wants to make amends to the people he hurt. Of course, that could take him a few years. He lives in Hawaii with his new wife and a daughter, although I'm not sure how that works since he never divorced his first wife."

"What does your sister say about him?"

"She hasn't seen him yet. Her family wanted to take their vacation first on Maui in case things don't work out with him."

"If he has changed and Kate forgives him, will you contact him?"

He clenched his fists under the table. Kate could forgive and forget all she wanted, but why drag him into it? "Why should I? The man made my childhood a living hell."

She sipped her tea and ran her finger along a bead of moisture on the side of the glass. "If he turned his life around and is making amends, it might do you good to forgive him. To err is human…"

He put his head in his hands, his shoulders shaking.

She reached across the table and touched his arm. "Justin?"

Raising his head, his laughter consumed him.

She gasped. "Why, you…you're laughing."

He wiped his eyes. "You are such a Pollyanna. I dubbed you that the first day I met you. 'To err is human.' What a load of—"

She warned, "Watch it."

He snorted. "Do you really believe all that crap you spew?"

She laughed with him, and the sound spilled over, bubbling toward him and sweeping him along in her world. He scoffed, but he could believe anything with her sitting across the table, could even believe he might forgive his old man.

Just as they finished their lunch, his cell phone chirped, bringing them back to his world…with a bullet. It was Victoria.

"So you escaped certain death a second time. You must've done something right in your previous life."

Victoria choked back a sob. "This is no joke, Justin. You have to get to that tunnel, bring in other agents and the Border Patrol, then destroy it."

He sneered, "Are you just coming to that conclusion now? Are you working with Leo?"

She took a shuddering breath. "Was."

His chest constricted. Another father figure up in smoke. "How far are you into this plot?"

"I'm not in it at all. Not anymore. Even before I saw you yesterday, I told Leo I wanted out. Told him I had enough."

Lila mouthed words at him, and he shook his head. He said to Victoria, "Is that why you ran yesterday? He shot at you, too."

She hissed through her teeth. "I'm on the run now. I argued with him, and he sensed betrayal."

Don't we all? His stomach churned. "Did you arrange to have Chad killed?"

She cried, "I swear, I didn't know they were going to kill Chad. Leo told me they were just supposed to follow him until he led them to the tunnel."

"Who's 'they'? Who are you working with?"

She whispered, "Al Tariq."

Justin almost choked on the bile rising in his gut. Leo working with Al Tariq.

He spit out, "What did you expect them to do with Chad once he led them to the tunnel? Slap his hands and tell him to go away and forget about it?

"I didn't know."

His voice hardened. "Who else?"

She whispered through her tears, "That I don't know."

"You don't know a lot. What happened at the compound that night?"

She drew in another shaky breath. "Prasad left. I couldn't stop him without appearing suspicious. Leo said we could deal with him later. So I disarmed the security and left."

He growled, "Left your colleagues to be murdered."

"I didn't realize they were going to kill everyone."

He said dryly, "Oh, just me?"

"They want the woman, Lila."

Justin's blood chilled as it crept through his veins, his eyes boring into Lila. He pushed the word out of his mouth. "Why?"

"To show them where the tunnel is."

One suspicion confirmed. "Don't they know? What about the men who murdered Chad?"

Her laugh, high and hysterical, flooded his ear. "The coyotes killed them. Leo never heard from them again after they told him they'd picked up Chad's trail."

He shot back, "How do you know they just didn't betray Leo? Now that he's given them information, they have no use for him."

"I don't think so. Other members of Al Tariq have contacted him since."

"How'd they track Lila to my place, and why'd they remove the dead body from the trunk?"

"They picked up Chad's car at the border crossing. Figured the woman driving his car either witnessed his murder or knew something about the tunnel. They followed her from the border. I guess the fact that she went to you didn't surprise Leo."

Victoria denied any knowledge of the man in the trunk, but revealed that they knew about Chad's meeting with an informant. Wrong place, wrong time for that informant.

Justin pressed. "Why, Victoria? Why did Leo become a traitor?"

She sighed. "The oldest reason in the book. Money."

"And you? Don't tell me love. I just ate lunch."

"Love? Leo doesn't know the meaning of the word."

"Is that why you want out now? He's not going to leave his wife for you after all?"

"How do you know about that?"

He drawled, "Let's just say I have my sources. You may have snowed me, but others knew."

She mumbled, "The son of a bitch ruined my marriage, but wanted to protect his own."

He snorted. "So this confession is all about a woman scorned?"

She paused. "It's more than that, Justin. I just thought Al Tariq wanted to use the tunnel to get more men into the country, set up more cells. I didn't realize they already had a specific objective."

Her excuses made his blood chill. What did she think Al Tariq planned to do once it had more cells in the country?

He prompted. "And? What's the plan?"

Victoria's next words roared in his ears, blotting out

the blue sky, dimming the sun, turning the cool breeze onto needles on his flesh.

He finished talking and dropped his cell phone on the table between them. His face, tight with fear must have alarmed Lila because her sharp words sliced through his fog.

"What's the matter, Justin?"

They had no time to lose, and Lila was in this as deeply as he was. She had to know the truth.

"Victoria told me why Al Tariq is so anxious to find this tunnel."

Lila sucked in her breath. "Why?"

"Al Tariq already has a plan, down to the men destined to carry it out, but we tossed most of them out of the country for visa violations last year. They want back in, and that tunnel's going to be their means."

Lila clutched the tablecloth. "What is it, Justin? What's their scheme?"

He stared above her head at the sea beyond them, and then locked his eyes on hers. "Al Tariq plans to launch an attack next month during the World Series."

Chapter Nine

Lila clapped her hands over her mouth. Every muscle in her body seized up as the horror of Justin's words assaulted her. The World Series started next month, and she and Tyler planned to be there, along with tens of thousands of others. She swept her palms across her face as if to clear away the image his words provoked.

Gripping the table, she choked out, "The World Series?"

Justin lifted a stiff shoulder. "Al Tariq is going to use that tunnel to provide passage, not only for the men, but the materials, and they need to do it quickly."

She unclenched her jaw to ask, "H-how are you going to stop them?"

"We have to find the tunnel and destroy it. And we have to stop Leo."

And destroy him?

She released her grip on the table and spread her hands. "Can you do that?"

"Victoria's providing the proof. Always thinking ahead, she recorded some of their pillow talk. I guess they discussed the best way to betray their country and their fellow agents while they were in bed." His eyes glinted with sparks of fury.

Lila shivered, despite the warmth of the sun on her back. Justin Vidal was a dangerous man to cross.

She cleared her throat. "Can you trust Victoria?"

"No, but I have no choice right now. I can't take Leo down without proof. Washington turns a blind eye to much of what we do, but it won't sanction indiscriminate elimination of HIA agents without evidence."

She jerked back. "Elimination?"

A deep sigh rumbled from his chest. "Forget it, Lila. You don't belong in this world."

Dropping her eyes from the resignation in his, she said, "But I *am* in it."

He grabbed her hand. "I wish to God you weren't. I wish you'd never accepted that ride from Chad."

The pressure of his hand on hers brought tears to her eyes, but she left it there, exulting in his touch.

She whispered, "If I'd never accepted that ride…" She looked up into his eyes.

He almost threw her hand across the table and said savagely, "Yeah, that, too."

She'd gone too far, but she got her answer. He felt it, too. This bond between them owed more to just the danger they'd shared this past week. He felt it but regretted it.

And did she regret it? She only knew she wanted to be in his arms, feel his kiss on her lips. Take him inside her, wholly and completely.

She blinked and took a sip of iced tea, the ice tinkling in the trembling glass. "What happens now?"

"I meet with Victoria, get the goods on Leo and

report both of them to Washington. Victoria's giving herself up, taking the consequences. Then I plan to meet Molina in Mexico, find the tunnel and call in the Border Patrol and the CIA. If we can stop Al Tariq from finishing and using that tunnel, I think we can avert the attack."

He made it all sound so easy. She asked the question hanging in the air, "And what about me?"

He took the hand he'd previously tossed aside, rubbing his thumb along the back of it. "Once Victoria and Leo are out of circulation and we find this tunnel, you'll be safe. You'll get your son back. You'll finish your research."

And I'll never see you again. Her heart thumped painfully against her rib cage. She returned the pressure of his hand, and their fingers entwined.

Before the hurt overwhelmed her, she switched gears. "When are you meeting with Victoria?"

"Tomorrow."

"Am I coming along?"

He ground out, "Absolutely not."

Narrowing her eyes, she said, "So there is some danger involved."

"There's always some danger involved, and this time you're not going to be in the middle of it."

HE SHIFTED on the couch and dug his fists into the cushions. Another night of her sleeping in his bed while he slept out here on the couch. He'd be glad when they got to Mexico. Although the sexual tension between them wouldn't lessen in a foreign country, at least he could work it off by keeping busy, keeping focused on the task before him.

Somehow his drive to find the tunnel was mixed up with his feelings for Lila. And that signaled danger.

He'd discovered long ago that emotional attachments interfered with his brand of justice. He wanted to see his father suffer for his treatment of his family, but when Justin made him pay, his mother turned on him.

His job with the HIA made it easy. He could deliver justice to scores of anonymous people and never have to engage them individually. Never have to face whether they appreciated it or him. Never have to open himself up and reveal his emotions only to get kicked in the teeth.

He screwed his eyes shut thinking about that lunch yesterday. The sun. The ocean breeze. Lila across from him, laughing. Her smile alone banished years of mistrust and pain from his psyche. Gave him hope.

Victoria's phone call had ruined it, brought him back to reality. His reality. Leo's betrayal stung. He'd mentored all of them—Fletch, Molina, himself. True, he'd never let Leo in completely, but then he never let anyone in completely.

Except Lila.

He shook his head and rolled off the couch. The water running in the bathroom told him she'd already gotten up and claimed the shower first. He pulled on his jeans from yesterday and started the coffee.

"Mmm, that smells good."

He turned with a mug in his hand. "You want some?"

She nodded, her curls still wet from the shower, brushing her shoulders. The rich smell of the coffee couldn't mask the floral scent emanating from her. He inhaled it and the natural beauty before him.

"Lots of milk, little sugar."

He turned back to the kitchen counter to fill her order. "I remember."

As he handed her the mug of steaming coffee, her eyes skimmed down his bare chest and got caught at the crotch of his jeans. He spun back toward the counter to pour himself a cup of coffee. Damn. He had less control than a teenage boy.

He said over his shoulder, "Did you leave me any hot water?"

A laugh tugged at her words. "A little. Lots of cold water though."

Walking right into her trap, he said, "I don't need a cold shower."

"Don't you?" Her delicate brows arched.

Coffee sprayed back into his cup midsip. Taking his coffee with him, he trudged past her toward the bathroom. "I'm going to take that shower now. A warm one."

He shut the bathroom door on her giggle. The attraction between then only confused things. The spray from the shower engulfing him did nothing to ease his hard desire for her.

She needed to get away from all this. Away from him. What could he offer her?

While Lila munched toast in the kitchen, he placed a call to Fletch, who ran a security company that employed off-duty cops. Justin arranged to have Fletch deploy a couple of armed men to watch the house…just in case.

He returned to the living room and loaded his Glock and slid it into his shoulder holster. He attached a sheath knife to his belt loop and buttoned a loose denim shirt over everything.

Watching his actions, she asked, "Where are you meeting?"

He crossed his arms. "You don't need to know that."

She scowled. "I'm not going to follow you." Tossing him the keys to the sports car, she said, "Take Matt's car."

He gestured to the black Porsche parked at the curb. "That's not your car?"

Shaking her head, she said, "I drive something a little more modest."

His brows collided over his nose. "Did you buy that for Matt?"

She laughed. "Don't look so thunderous. He bought that with his own money—endorsements before the accident. He likes me to drive it for him to keep it running smoothly. He loves that car."

He rubbed his chin. "It's a little conspicuous."

"It's a lot fast," she retorted. "I mean, in case you have to make a run for it."

He accepted the offer. "What are you going to do this morning?"

She opened her eyes wide. "Am I allowed to leave the house?"

As much as he wanted to keep her under lock and key, he figured she was safe here, especially with Fletch's guys on the lookout. "I asked Fletch to send over a few men to watch the house. They're going to be in a white car across the street. You should be okay here. Nobody knows where this place is, anyway."

She countered, "Brooke does."

"Yeah, I had her and Molina over a few times for dinner. Fletch, too."

"And Fletch's wife?"

He nodded. What was she getting at?

Brushing crumbs off the table into her hand, she asked, "Were you the odd man out, or was it couples only?"

Did she care? "Couples only."

She pierced him with her blue gaze. "Did she know about the HIA?"

He feigned ignorance. "Who?"

She gritted her teeth. "Your date."

She did care. "No."

"That must've been awkward for her with the five of you in on the joke."

He answered, "Fletch's wife doesn't know."

She stood up and dumped her plate in the sink. "So what happened to her?"

He opened his mouth as she spun around. "Your date, I mean."

Lifting one shoulder, he said, "She left."

Lila let out a long breath and stood with her back leaning against the sink.

He liked her jealousy. He couldn't help himself. "You done with the interrogation?"

A slow flush stained her cheeks pink. "I'm sorry."

He wasn't. He waved his hand. "You never answered me. What are you going to do this morning?"

"Maybe start packing for Mexico. Maybe take a book to the beach."

He bit the inside of his cheek. If she went to the beach, Fletch's men would have to follow her. "Whatever you do, be careful. Lock the doors behind me when I leave and don't open up to anyone. If you do go down to the beach, let the guys out in front know and be aware of your surroundings."

She spread her arms out to encompass the nearly bare room. "I thought this was your safe house."

Nodding, he said, "It is, but you can't be too careful."

She flashed one of his spy novels at him. "I'll read this and get some pointers."

He laughed. He did that a lot in her company.

Standing before her, ready to go, he held out Fletcher Bale's card. "If I don't come back today, call Fletch."

She put her hands behind her back and dropped her head. "Don't say that."

He took one of her wrists and put the card in her hand. "Just in case."

Her hair created a veil over her face, and he reached out and placed one finger beneath her chin, raising her head.

Tears shimmered in her enormous blue eyes. Tears for him? Her bottom lip quivered, and he lowered his mouth to stop it. Sliding his tongue along the seam of her lips, he tasted the salt as her tears spilled down her cheeks.

He hooked an arm around her waist, dragging her closer, and she responded by wrapping her arms around his neck. Pressing his body full length along hers, he devoured her mouth. Her tears became his as their wetness dampened his face.

He ended the kiss and pulled her head down onto his shoulder. Entangling his fingers in her hair, he murmured against her silky curls, "Its okay. It's all going to work out." Even if he didn't quite believe it himself, he had to convince her.

Sniffling, she raised her head to look into his eyes. He swept her up in his arms and carried her to his bedroom. He settled her on the bed, sitting on its edge.

Her curls clung to her wet face, and he stroked them back. She closed her eyes and he studied her moist lips, parted in expectation. He couldn't do this. He rose from the bed, but she reached out to grab his wrist and whispered, "Don't leave me."

She released his wrist and ran her hand up his thigh, caressing the rough material of his jeans. She rubbed the palm of her hand over his hard desire and moaned, "I need you."

He needed her, too. What if he never came back from his meeting with Victoria?

He stretched out next to Lila on the bed and skimmed his hands down the length of her body, caressing each curve. She trembled beneath his touch and drew closer. She yanked at the buttons on his shirt and peeled it from his chest.

The weapons beneath his shirt served as an unwelcome reminder of the task ahead. He unhooked his holster and his sheath, and placed them on the floor, out of sight, before pulling his T-shirt over his head.

The air hissed between his teeth, as she trailed her fingernails down to his belly and hooked her fingers in the waistband of his jeans. He tugged on the buttons and pulled the jeans off along with his boxers.

He exposed his naked body to her and she drank it in slowly, her eyes roaming the length of him. Her intimate gaze felt like a caress, and he hardened fully in response.

Reaching forward, he unfastened the small buttons of her blouse until it lay open revealing a white lacy bra. He pulled the blouse from her shoulders, and unhooked her bra in the back. Her breasts tumbled forward, her nipples like pearls in their eagerness for his touch.

He lowered his mouth to her breast, running his tongue over one dusky pearl. Clasping her hands behind his head, she arched her back, and he took the sweet invitation. His tongue flicked to her other breast, and she gasped, hooking her leg around his hip. His erection pressed against her, and she reached down and took him in her hands. Her thumb encircled his tip, and he groaned with need.

His mouth closed around hers, his tongue exploring its sweet darkness. She inched closer, as if to meld her body with his, her light skirt still blocking their ultimate connection.

He released her lips and kissed her ear, her neck, the hollow of her throat where her pulse beat steadily, setting the pace of their love making.

Sliding her skirt down over her hips, he hooked his fingers in her panties, slipping them over the curve of her buttocks and down her legs.

It was his turn now. He eased her onto her back and soaked in her beautiful body, her skin glowing with a desire that sent a surge through his veins. She whimpered and rolled towards him. Pressing his body against hers, his arousal thrust between her thighs. Her legs fell open, and he traced his fingers along the opening to her feminine essence. Letting out a long sigh, she pushed against his fingers and he slid them inside.

"Please, Justin, I need you closer. I need all of you inside me."

He rolled on top of her. While he kissed her lips, he entered her, and she accepted him fully, wrapping her legs around his hips.

Their bodies rose and fell together, each riding the

same swell of need and desire. Her arms tightened around his back as she reached the pinnacle of her passion. As he felt her warmth spread, he cried out with his release, filling her with his life-affirming seed.

They lay together, legs entwined, as he wrapped one of her curls around his finger. He wanted to hold her in his arms forever and keep her safe.

"I have to leave now."

"I know. Be careful. I can't lose you, Justin."

BEFORE HE pulled away from the house, he took note of the two men slouched in the white car across the street. They flashed the agreed-upon signal, Justin blew out a breath, sinking into the low leather seat.

As Justin took the turns leading to the zoo, the Porsche growled beneath him, responsive to his slightest touch. Like Lila.

The feel of her beneath his lips, his fingertips, infused every cell in his body with hot, pulsing desire.

If meeting with Victoria didn't mean getting one step closer to keeping Lila safe, he would've canceled the meeting, stayed with Lila and made slow, sinuous love to her all afternoon.

He punched the accelerator, and the powerful car roared forward. First things first.

Ambling through the zoo, he took a circuitous route to the reptile house. The cool darkness enfolded him as he entered the building. He glanced at the benches stationed between the glass cases as he circled the exhibits.

A group of children squealed. He jerked his head around. The kids pointed, mouths agape, at a huge boa unfurling itself from around a rock. Its cold eyes seemed to pin him down, its tongue flicking in and out of its mouth.

Of all the places to meet. She couldn't pick the monkeys?

Turning the next corner, he saw a lone woman seated on the bench in the middle of the room. She stared down at a zoo map in her lap, her head bent over, a large hat concealing her face. The black hair that hung forward and the long legs stretching in front of her were unmistakably Victoria's.

She didn't look up at his approach. Didn't move. He crouched down next to her.

Drip.

Drip.

Dark droplets landed on the sodden map. Placing his hand on her hat, he tipped her head back.

A gaping grin slashed her throat from one end to the other. He dropped her head, and her body slumped to the side. He scanned the bench and the ground around her. Nothing. No bag, no purse, no tapes. No proof.

He heaved himself up, his gut churning. Staggering toward the exit of the reptile house, he bashed his shoulder against the corner of a display case. The green viper inside slid down the tree and lunged at the glass, forked tongue spitting out of its mouth.

Bursting outside, Justin gulped the air as he broke into a trot. He rested his hand on his gun as he kept his head down and made for the exit.

He didn't need a fast car to escape. No one waited in the reptile house for him. No one followed him. Were they giving up on him? Conceding defeat? No, not defeat, just hatching another plan.

If Victoria told the truth, Leo and Al Tariq didn't know the location of the tunnel. But they were betting Lila did. The thought made him take the Porsche through its paces on the freeway. How could he keep her safe with no proof of Leo's involvement?

He should take out Leo now, worry about the proof later. His hands gripped the black leather of the steering wheel. His blood hammered his temples.

By the time he pulled up in front of the house, his breath raked through his lungs. As he scrambled out of the car, he swung the door open so fast and hard it banged back on his leg.

The two men from Fletch's company beeped the horn in acknowledgment, and Justin waved them off. His long stride covered the distance from the curb to the porch in four steps, and he burst through the front door.

Lila, curled on the couch with a book, looked up as he charged into the room. She rose from the couch, her eyes searching his face. "It didn't go well?"

At the sight of her, he drew in a deep breath and exhaled slowly. She was safe. "Victoria's dead."

Lila's face paled as she wrapped her arms around her body, hugging herself.

His brow furrowed as he delivered more bad news. "And I didn't get any proof on Leo."

She rasped out, "Was it a trap?"

Passing a hand over his face, he said, "For me? I don't know. I don't think so. Nobody ambushed me. But if she had the tapes with her, someone took them."

He didn't mention how Victoria died. Lila didn't need that image in her head.

"She was dead when you got there?"

He sank down on the couch and massaged his neck. "Yeah. I never even got the chance to talk to her."

Settling beside him, she took his hand and rubbed the rough spots with her fingertips. "What can you do without proof that Leo's the traitor?"

"I'll just have to beat him to that tunnel." He squeezed her hand. "We're going to Mexico now."

"Right this minute?" Her eyes widened as her hand jerked his.

"We don't have any more time to lose. Even though I have nothing on Leo, we still have a better idea of where the tunnel is than he does. Hopefully, Brooke got the message to Molina, and he'll meet us there. When this is all over you can go home, Lila. Get your son back. Get your life back."

She looked up at him, her smile not quite reaching her eyes. "But before that, we have a job to do."

Did she realize once that job was over, they'd have to say goodbye? He had no room for her in his life, and she deserved the biggest space anyone could carve out for her.

They spent the next half hour throwing a few things in a bag, avoiding conversation, avoiding each other's touch. He'd been a fool to make love to her.

Before they walked out the door, Lila's cell phone rang. She checked the display and grimaced, holding up her hand to Justin.

She turned her back to him. "Hello… What are you talking about, Gareth? Stop yelling."

Justin waited with his hand on the doorknob. Damn that ex-husband of hers.

She choked, and he spun around. She still had her back to him, her shoulders hunched forward.

She screamed into the phone, "You're lying. You're lying to me."

He caught her as she swayed backward. Collapsing against his chest, she crumpled to the floor and dropped the phone.

Kneeling down next to her, he grabbed her trembling hands. "What's wrong?"

She lifted her face to him, and he recoiled from the anguish etched in every feature

"They took Tyler."

Chapter Ten

Lila grasped the floor, digging her fingers into the carpet so she wouldn't fall off. The tinny sound of Gareth's voice, demanding, accusing, clicked at her from the phone on the floor. Nausea surged through her body, and she retched.

Through a spinning vortex of misery, she saw Justin bend forward and pick up the phone. He pulled her up to the couch where she huddled, a boneless, quivering mass. His low voice rumbled, vibrating against her ear as he held her head against his chest.

The words he spoke into the phone tumbled over her, making no sense. Her thoughts swirled around one bitter kernel of truth. They had Tyler.

Gareth had accused her of hiring a man to kidnap Tyler from him. As soon as he'd uttered the words, she knew who had taken Tyler, but she didn't understand why.

Justin put the phone down and sat silently stroking her hair. She stirred. As much as she wanted to, she couldn't lie here against his chest trying to block out Gareth's words.

Raising her head, she looked into his face, creased with concern.

He asked, "Are you ready to hear?"

She covered her face with her hands but nodded.

He took a deep breath. "The man who took Tyler said you ordered him to do so. Your son didn't believe it and put up a fight. The housekeeper didn't much believe it, either. When they left, she called your ex-husband."

She clenched her hands in her lap. "It's them, isn't it?"

"Probably."

Pounding her fist against her thigh, she cried, "Why? What do they want with my little boy?"

Grabbing her wrists, he said, "They don't want him. They want you."

She yanked her hands out of his grasp. "Then why not take me? Why him? Why my little boy?" Her eyes burned with unshed tears.

He jumped up. "We've been too successful. They can't find you. Leo doesn't know where this house is. They haven't been able to follow us."

She lashed out, "I don't care about that anymore. I just want my son back."

He raked a hand through his hair. "I don't understand how they tracked down Tyler. How'd they connect him to you? How'd they connect your ex with you? You said you kept your maiden name, right?"

She didn't understand the importance of that now. Tyler was gone. Throwing her hands out, she said, "I guess everyone in San Diego knows Gareth Stone."

Justin spun on his heel. "Gareth Stone of Touch-Stone is your ex-husband?"

Standing up, she faced the blaze in his eyes. "Yes."

The fire went out, and he groaned. "Why didn't you tell me this before?"

Scowling, she said, "Why should I? What difference does it make?"

His tone measured, he stated, "It's like you said, 'everyone in San Diego knows Gareth Stone.' Any information they get on Lila Monroe is going to contain a link back to Gareth Stone and TouchStone. Any information on Gareth Stone is going to include the fact that he has a son with his ex-wife."

Her knees buckled, and he swooped in to catch her. Sobbing, she said, "I put my son's life in danger. Gareth's right. It's my fault."

He held her and soothed, "It's not your fault. You didn't know who Chad was. You didn't realize what you were you up against when you left that clearing and came to me."

She pushed away from him. "I have to get him back. I'll give this Leo Caine anything he asks."

Holding up his hands, he said, "Slow down. He hasn't asked for anything yet."

She cut in, "But he will. Call him. Call him now."

"He'll call us when he's ready. We have to go down to San Diego and see your ex-husband, talk to his housekeeper. Figure out if they left any message when they snatched Tyler."

A knife twisted in her gut at the words, and she put a hand on the couch to steady herself. He made a move toward her, but she swept her hand forward to hold him off. She had to be strong. If she had to do this on her own, she would. What would Justin Vidal care about her son if he could beat Leo to the tunnel?

He drew back from her, his eyes flickering. "Your ex threatened to call the police, and we can't have that. If the police get involved now…"

She jumped in, "They'll kill Tyler." The words tasted bitter in her mouth, but she had to confront the truth head-on. She didn't really blame her mother for her Dad's death, she blamed herself. Her love hadn't been strong enough to protect him. It had to be enough for Tyler.

Justin clamped the back of his neck with his hand and rolled his head. "We don't know that for sure, but it's best for me to handle the situation right now. If Leo didn't leave a message at your ex-husband's house, he'll be in contact."

SILENCE REIGNED in the car during the half-hour drive down to Stone's house in La Jolla. *La jolla* meant *the jewel* in Spanish, and it was, a sparkling emerald glittering on a sapphire coast. Matt's Porsche hugged the hills and turns, winding through the streets where opulent homes hung back coyly behind velvet lawns.

They rolled up to a security gate, Justin remarking, "This didn't do much good today."

He buzzed the intercom, and a man's voice scratched over the speaker. "Who is it?"

"It's Justin Vidal. I have Lila with me."

The wrought iron gate rolled open, and Justin eased the car through, curving along the circular driveway.

He felt Lila tense beside him. Did this house hold unpleasant memories for her?

A generously proportioned Latina answered the door, her face tearstained and swollen. Throwing herself at Lila, she sobbed, "I'm so sorry, Missus Lila. The man pushed me. Before I knew what he was doing, he grabbed Tyler. I screamed at him, but he hit my face."

Lila touched the bruise on the woman's face. "It's not your fault, Graciela."

"Damn right it's not." A tall man approached them, his arctic blue eyes glittering, his thin lips a hard line.

He thrust his hand out toward Justin. "Vidal? I'm Gareth Stone. Are you going to tell me what the hell is going on and who took my son? If they want money, I'll give them whatever they ask. I can have millions at my disposal as early as tomorrow afternoon."

Justin returned Stone's firm grasp, taking in the man's expensive clothes. Looked pretty much like the pictures he'd seen of him in the papers, except that man was smiling. Despite his welcoming gesture, this man was pissed off.

Expensive perfume drifted into the room as a tall, elegant woman glided in its wake. Her voice, like cool water, poured out, "I'm sorry this happened, Lila. You must feel so…terrified."

Lila stood with her arm around Graciela. "We're here to find out what happened and get Tyler back."

The woman floated up to Justin. "You must be Mr. Vidal. I'm Liz Stone, Tyler's stepmother."

From her corner of the room, Lila snorted.

Justin took the cool fingers, which were withdrawn immediately. The Stones looked as if they'd just stepped out of a magazine.

Liz Stone turned to her husband. "Let's go into the living room and sit down, Gareth, and sort this out. Graciela, bring us some refreshments, please."

Before she left the room, Graciela whispered in

Lila's ear and Lila squeezed her hand. Then they made their way into the living room.

The Stones sat next to each other on a white brocade sofa, while Lila took a straight-backed chair to the left of them. Justin perched uneasily on the edge of another chair that looked so minimalist, he was afraid he'd break it.

The couple on the couch looked at him with raised brows. He began, "The people who took Tyler are involved with a terrorist organization."

Stone guffawed and then stopped when he looked into Justin's eyes. "You're not joking."

Justin said, "I wouldn't joke about something this serious."

Both sets of eyes pinned Lila in their gaze. She straightened her back and stared them down.

Justin rubbed a hand along his jaw. This wasn't going to be easy. "I work for a government agency formed specifically to track these people down. It's imperative right now you don't call the police. That could put Tyler in danger."

Stone spit out, "I think Tyler's already in danger."

Justin amended, "Greater danger. Anything you can tell me about the kidnapping would be helpful."

Shaking his head, Stone said, "I don't know much. Liz and I left for work this morning, leaving Tyler in Graciela's care." He glanced at Lila. "She's watched him many times before."

Lila stared straight ahead, still, except for fingers drumming the arm of the chair.

Stone said, "Graciela called me as soon as the man left with Tyler. That was about four o'clock?" He looked to his wife, and she nodded.

"Graciela told me the man said he was there on Lila Monroe's orders, but she didn't believe that."

Lila intoned, "You did."

"I wish it had been that," he snapped back.

Justin interrupted the exchange. "I'm curious. Why didn't Graciela call the police right away?"

Shrugging, Stone replied, "In case there was any truth to what the man said about Lila, she didn't want to cause any trouble for her."

Stone folded his arms. "My housekeeper has a certain loyalty to my ex-wife."

Graciela walked across the white-marble tiles carrying a tray laden with coffee, little sandwiches and cakes. Lila jumped up to help her place the tray on the glass coffee table.

Stone gestured toward Graciela. "You can ask her what happened."

Justin said, "Sit down, Graciela. I'd like to ask you some questions about the kidnapping."

She sat in a chair close to Lila's and nodded. In answer to Justin's questions, she explained how the man buzzed the intercom telling her he had to deliver something to Mr. Stone, which wasn't unusual. When she opened the door, he barreled into her while another man waited on the porch. He said he was there to get Tyler for his mother, that Lila was waiting for him in the car.

Graciela put a hand to her cheek. "When I told him I wanted to see Missus Lila, he smacked my face. Tyler was playing with his new cell phone and came into the hallway when he heard the commotion."

She sniffled. "He saw the man hit me, and rushed up to stop him."

Justin's gut clenched. "What did the man do?"

Dropping her head and heaving her shoulders, she said, "He knocked Tyler in the head, and Tyler fell over."

Lila rocketed from her chair. "You didn't tell me the man hurt him. Oh my God." She started pacing the floor, her hands covering her mouth.

Graciela said, "I'm sorry, Missus Lila. I didn't want to tell you. If that man hadn't knocked him out, Tyler would've fought him off. He's a big boy now."

Justin's eyes shifted to Lila, who collapsed back into the chair. He fought the impulse to go to her and take her in his arms. She didn't seem to want that from him anyway. Pushed him away at the house.

He returned his attention to Graciela. "So the man carried him out of the house."

The woman nodded, tears running down her plump cheeks.

"Why didn't you call the police?"

She knotted her hands. "I—I thought just in case Missus Lila did take Tyler." She paused. Looking into Justin's eyes, she heaved a sigh. "And, *señor,* I'm not legal."

Stone glared at her. "He doesn't need to know that."

Justin ignored him. "Graciela, did the man say anything else? Leave anything behind? A note?"

She shook her head. "Nothing, *señor.*"

"Did you get a look at his car? The license plate?"

"I ran outside and saw him drive away in a medium-size dark car. It didn't have license plates. I looked."

Justin blew out a breath. What was Leo's game? Did he want to trade Tyler for Lila? Not if *he* had anything to say about it.

Stone interrupted his thoughts. "We've told you what we know. Now it's your turn. Why is this terrorist group interested in my son? And what were you doing with Lila when I called her?"

Justin replied, "That's not important. I'll get Tyler back."

Jumping up, Stone yelled, "Damn you. I want to know. I want to know what harebrained escapade my ex-wife's gotten into this time."

Lila pressed back against the chair, her mouth compressed into a thin line.

Justin pushed out of the uncomfortable chair and stood over Stone, looking down at him with narrowed eyes. "I told you. That's not important now, and I'm not at liberty to discuss the details with you."

Stone stalked over to Lila's chair, and she jerked back from him.

He sneered, "Don't let the act fool you, Vidal. She's hard as nails. Who do you think helped me build up TouchStone? Beneath the blond earth-goddess facade lurks one shrewd businesswoman. But she has a weakness. Too trusting. She'll try to rescue every stray dog that crosses her path. In the end, it was bad for business."

Justin stood rooted to the floor. So this was Lila's secret. She pretended she got her money from the divorce, that it had been her ex's money, when actually she was entitled to that money. The man sunk further in his estimation. And Lila rose.

Stone continued, "This is your fault, isn't it, Lila?"

She winced, and Justin felt his blood percolate.

Stone said, "What was it this time? You picked up

some lonely terrorist by the side of the road? Did you smuggle weapons for him?"

He laughed. "My lawyer's going to be very interested in this story when we sue you to get sole custody of Tyler."

A strangled cry rose from Lila's throat, and Justin tightened his fists.

Stone jeered, "How does it feel to be responsible for your son's kidnapping?"

It took Justin just two strides to get to Lila's tormentor. He clamped his hand on the back of Stone's neck, yanking him away from Lila's chair. Stone dangled for a moment like a puppet on a string before Justin landed his fist against his whitened teeth.

A woman screamed.

Stone staggered back, his hands clamped over his mouth, his eyes wide. Justin scored another punch somewhere above Stone's hands. Blood spurted from his nose, and he dropped to the floor.

Like a coiled spring, Justin's fist drew back again, his rage roaring in his ears. A hand rested on his bicep, and he turned and looked down into Lila's blue eyes, warmed to a deep hue. That warmth pulled him back from the brink of his cascading wrath.

He dropped his fist. Liz, riveted by the violence, remained on the sofa, while Graciela crouched over Stone. A spray of blood marred the marble tiles.

Plucking at his sleeve, Lila whispered, "Let's go."

Once outside, he opened the car door for her and slid in the other side. Rubbing his knuckles, he said, "I'm sorry."

She snapped her seat belt. "For what?"

"For losing control. I try not to let that happen."

Lifting her shoulders, she said, "How's your hand?"

He gunned the engine and shot out of the gate. "Sore."

All conversation ceased on the ride back to Justin's house in Encinitas. A cold house, just like Stone's, but in a different way. Only Lila had the power to infuse it with warmth, and now her inner light was extinguished.

She wrapped some ice in a towel and pressed it to his knuckles. "That scene must've reminded you of your father."

He swallowed. That thought hadn't occurred to him at the time. His need to protect Lila drove him. The guy was unbelievable. He ended his marriage to this incredible woman over business?

He shrugged, and she looked away.

"How did you end up married to a man like that?"

Rubbing her eyes, she said, "He wasn't like that in college. He was full of enthusiasm and ideas. He had a plan to start a new company to store data for other companies. He carried me along with his zeal, and when we graduated we borrowed some money and started the business. We spent so much time together on the business, marriage came naturally. We ran off to Vegas."

He grinned. "Figures."

"We started making lots of money, and it changed him. It's amazing what the desire for money can do to people."

Justin agreed, thinking of Leo.

She continued, "He started taking shortcuts, which compromised the data, without telling the customers. I found out and threatened to expose him."

Shaking his head, he said, "He ended the marriage over a business disagreement?"

"It was more than a disagreement, Justin. It spoke to his character. Besides, the marriage had ended long before that. He never wanted to be a father to Tyler."

Clouds rolled across her face, and he longed to banish them. "Sounds like Tyler has a lot of guts. Just like his mom."

She threw him a watery smile. "D-do you think that man might've killed him when he hit him?"

"No. They won't hurt him. Leo won't hurt him."

She returned, "Unless I don't do what he says. Why doesn't he call and let us know what he wants?"

Justin's phone rang, and Lila jumped. Checking the display, he shook his head at her.

"Vidal here."

"Mr. Vidal, this is Pradeep Mansour, Prasad's father. Is Prasad with you?"

A deep sigh rumbled in Justin's chest. "No. He's not in the hospital?"

Mr. Mansour replied, "He left. His doctor just called me, and I thought he might be with you."

Justin assured him he wasn't and ended the call with a wrinkled brow. Damn fool. Did he want to make a run for Chad's title as most impulsive agent?

He speed-dialed Prasad's cell-phone number and got his voice mail. No surprise there. He snapped his phone shut.

"What is it now?" Lila asked.

He pocketed his phone. "Prasad left the hospital."

Drawing her hair back from her face, she asked, "Why? Where would he go?"

"I'm not sure, but I have an idea."

"Mexico?"

"Mexico."

The freckles stood out on her beautiful face, now drained of color and drawn tightly across her delicate bones. Her eyes, dark pools of misery and fear, claimed half her face.

The lines in his own face softened. "You look worn-out."

"What are we going to do? How are we going to get Tyler back?" Her slim fingers fluttered before she buried her face in her hands.

He wondered when the grief was going to hit her full force. She'd already run the gamut of emotions from denial to guilt. Her shoulders shook, but her tears fell silently.

"We'll get Tyler home safely." He dropped the towel onto the coffee table and rubbed Lila's back with his palm. "But first, we wait. I guarantee Leo will contact us with some deal, and when he does I'll bring the full force of my training and experience to bear on him, I'll find him, and I'll get Tyler back."

She closed her eyes and leaned against his shoulder, her hair clinging to his stubble. He cupped her face in his hand. "You're exhausted. I'm putting you to bed."

He swept her up in his arms and carried her to his bedroom where he tugged down the bed covers and placed her on the sheets. He plumped up a pillow beneath her head and turned to leave.

"Don't go, Justin." Her arms reached out for him, so he returned to her.

He kicked off his shoes, pulled his shirt over his head and slipped into the bed beside her. He wrapped his arms around her and kept watch until her deep breathing signaled she'd drifted off to sleep.

The next morning, the sun filtered through the slats of the blinds showering sunbeams on Lila's golden hair as it fanned out on the pillow. They still clung together. From the stiffness of his back, he knew they must've slept like that all night. Her hair tickled his chin, as she burrowed her head deeper into the hollow between his neck and shoulder.

He wanted to be the one responsible for smoothing away the lines etched around her eyes and mouth, for kissing her lips back into a smile. He had to get her son back for her. Unharmed.

This time he didn't seek justice for the nameless, faceless masses. He sought justice for Lila. And to hell with the risks posed to him.

She stirred and stretched. She inched her toes up his leg, and he swallowed. He wanted to make love to her all over again. He held back the other day, been gentle when he wanted to devour her, claim her as his own. But he had no right, so he allowed her to set the rhythm. She wanted comfort. That's all.

His cell phone gave a muffled ring, and he reached over to grab it from the pocket of his shirt crumpled on the floor. Lila sat up, eyes wide, urging him to hurry.

He answered after the second ring.

"Nice to know I can still reach you, Lone Wolf."

Chapter Eleven

Lila gathered the sheet around her, staring at Justin's muscled back, now ramrod straight.

He growled into the phone, "Bring the boy back."

Her heart pumped blood into her head so fast, the room swam before her. Leo. The man who took her son.

Still with his back to her, Justin said, "That's not going to happen."

She pulled at his arm, and he looked over his shoulder, putting his finger to his lips.

Speaking into the phone again, he barked, "Take me instead. I know where Chad died. I'll be more use to you in searching for that tunnel. I'll find it for you."

Sitting next to him on the bed, she gestured for the phone. She had to speak to Leo herself, had to plead for her son's life. She'd give Leo anything he wanted.

Justin said, "Let her talk to her son. We have to know he's okay."

He listened for a moment, and then handed the phone to her. She almost dropped it in her greediness.

Tyler's voice came over the line, sounding unnaturally high and young. "Mom?"

A spasm of fear clutched at her heart, but she took a deep breath. She had to be strong for him. Had to be strong for both of them. "Tyler, are you all right?"

"Yeah, I'm okay. I knew you didn't send that guy to Dad's house. I tried to fight him off, Mom. He hurt Graciela and I kicked him, but he hit me on the head. If he hadn't done that, I think I could've gotten away from him."

At least the ordeal hadn't stopped his normal flow of chatter. "How's your head?" Her hands shook so much, she had to hold on to the phone with both of them.

"I have a big bump, but I feel okay. Are you coming to get me, Mom?"

She stated, "Yes. Yes, I'm coming to get you soon. Are they treating you okay?"

He hiccupped. "Yeah, they gave me some hamburgers and I got to drink soda."

Laughing, she said, "Great, you're going to come back to me with cavities."

His laugh caught in his throat, and she clamped her lips tight to trap the scream that threatened to pry them open.

Tyler gulped. "Hurry, Mom."

A man's voice took his place. "Get Vidal back on the phone."

She cried, "Please don't hurt my son. I'll tell you where Chad died. I'll help you find the tunnel."

Justin snatched the phone from her hand. "If you hurt that boy, I'll kill you."

He listened for a minute more and then ended the call, dropping the phone on the bed.

Tears moistened her eyes, but she held them back. "What does he want us to do?"

Justin pulled on his shirt. Shoving the hair back from his face, he said, "He wants me to bring you to him in exchange for Tyler, and he wants to take you to Mexico so you can show him the spot where Chad died."

Blinking, she said, "He wants me to go to Mexico with him?"

He nodded. "That's his plan."

She bounded out of bed. "Let's go. My stuff's already packed. I'll call my mom to tell her to expect Tyler…"

Justin hadn't moved from the edge of the bed. She wedged her free hand on her hip. "What are you waiting for? Let's go."

Pushing off the bed, he said, "We're not going, Lila. At least you're not going."

A dull pain pressed against the base of her skull. He was signing her son's death warrant. "What do you mean?"

"I'll get Tyler back another way. I'm not turning you over to Leo. I'm not going to allow him to find that tunnel and carry out his Machiavellian plans with Al Tariq."

Stepping back from him, she said, "I'm not yours to 'turn over.'"

He winced. "I know that. I mean, there's a way to rescue Tyler without endangering you, too."

And without giving away the location of the tunnel. She dropped the sheet. "I'm listening."

He rubbed the stubble on his chin. "I don't have a plan yet, but—"

She stopped him. "Leo does have a plan, and he has

my son. I'm going with him to Mexico to show him that tunnel."

He made up the step between them. "How can Leo be sure you'll take him to the right location?"

She sucked in her lower lip. "You mean, once he sends Tyler home, he'll have nothing over me?"

"Exactly."

She answered her own question. "If he releases Tyler, I'll give him my word."

Justin's harsh laugh grated against her heart. "Do you think that's going to be good enough for Leo Caine? The man's a traitor to his country. You're going to trust him to keep his word?"

What bothered him more, that Leo betrayed his country or betrayed Justin Vidal? Tossing her hair back, she answered, "I have to trust him. There's no other way."

He reached out to her. "Trust me instead. I'm telling you there is another way. I'll find it. Once Leo gives me his location, I can go in and rescue Tyler."

Her nostrils flared. Too dangerous. "Leo must've warned you against doing that."

Dropping his arms, he looked away. "He did."

She pressed, "What did he say?" She steeled herself against the inevitable.

"He said he'd kill Tyler if you didn't come alone."

She covered her face and choked out, "You see? There's no other way."

She knew she'd have to go it alone. Knew it from the moment she heard about Tyler's kidnapping. This man standing in front of her knew nothing about love, not the kind of love she had for Tyler. He'd never known a mother's love. What could she expect from him? She was not going to endanger Tyler's life—any more than she already had.

He tried again. "There is a way, Lila. We've rescued hostages before. I can do it."

Another protest rose in her throat, and she swallowed it. Best to play his game for now. "How long do we have?"

His lean jaw relaxed. "He's giving us twenty-four hours, but once he gives me the location, he'll expect you to come in immediately, and I need time. I'll call him back just before the deadline expires, get his location and put my plan into action."

She forced herself to breathe deeply. "What are we going to do until then? I don't think I can hang on until tomorrow morning."

He gripped her shoulders. "You're just about the strongest woman I know, Lila Monroe. You can do it. In the meantime, I'm going to marshal what forces I can, and maybe you should change out of those clothes you slept in last night."

She looked down and pasted a grin on her face.

While she stood in the shower, she marshaled her own forces and made her own plans. She'd see Tyler within the next twenty-four hours without risking his life in some hostage situation.

As she soaped up with the washcloth, circling it over her body, she felt Justin's hands on her skin. She never expected he could be so gentle, and last night he offered the comfort she needed. He didn't even undress her, but he stayed with her and held her. When she woke up in the middle of the night, the dark shadows in the room amplified her fear for Tyler. But she nestled closer to Justin, and the fear receded.

His rage at Gareth surprised her until she recalled the circumstances of his father's departure. Justin must've felt as if he was rescuing his sister all over again. Even if he did it to exorcise past demons, she'd never had anyone stand up for her like that before.

She experienced a mean sort of pleasure when Justin brought Gareth down. Couldn't help it. Gareth was not the same man she'd married in front of an Elvis impersonator in Vegas. His and Liz's nuptials embodied every lavish wedding stereotype in *Modern Bride*. White horses. Glass Cinderella carriages. Doves. Tyler told her all about it, and they giggled over it together.

She gasped and sagged against the shower wall. Tyler.

Justin knocked on the bathroom door. "Are you okay?"

She called out, "Yeah, I'll be done in a minute."

They switched places, and she cooked some omelets for breakfast and made coffee. While they shared breakfast, he flipped between several morning-news programs.

He tossed the remote on the table. "Nothing about Victoria's death at the zoo."

Lila coughed around her orange juice. "The zoo? You met Victoria at the zoo?"

"The reptile house. Victoria had a flair for the dramatic."

"How'd she die?" After all, it might be her own fate.

He picked up their plates and turned to the sink. "You don't need to know that."

Why was he trying to keep things from her now? She

said, "It must have been some horrible way. And these people have Tyler."

He spun around. "I'll keep him safe. I'll keep you both safe."

Was he trying to convince her or himself? She changed the subject. "Have you tried calling Prasad?"

"I tried. He's not answering."

"How about Molina's girlfriend, Brooke?"

"I called her, and she gave Molina my message. I have a feeling we're all going to converge on Loma Vista at the same time."

Lila shivered. And then what? Things didn't go so well the last time everyone converged on Loma Vista. That last convergence resulted in at least four dead bodies. How many this time?

Justin spent the rest of the day either on his computer or on his cell phone. At least he'd gotten the Border Patrol interested. Since he couldn't give them the exact location of the tunnel or even verify its existence, they told him to call them when he got down there and could give them a precise location.

He had less luck with HIA headquarters in D.C. Leo had already warned headquarters about Lone Wolf, how his partner had been murdered in Mexico, how the HIA field office had been hit while he was there, how another agent had nearly been run over by a car in his presence and still another murdered at the zoo.

Lila listened to his account of his conversation with wide eyes. "They think you're responsible?"

He exhaled. "Leo doesn't have any proof, but then neither do I. We're equally under suspicion, which means I can't count on any help from headquarters."

"Didn't they investigate the massacre at the compound in the desert?"

"They did, but Leo didn't leave any evidence, and neither did Victoria. HIA knows it was an inside job, but believes I could be responsible just as much as anyone else." He shrugged. "I guess they have little faith in their agents."

She didn't tell him she had no faith in his ability to rescue Tyler on his own. She wouldn't have had faith in a whole army to rescue Tyler. That job belonged to Tyler's mother.

As the day limped into night, Justin convinced her to go out to dinner, but conversation dragged and appetites waned. The deadline drew near and hung over every bite.

They each got ready for bed, and Lila watched from a crack in the bathroom door as Justin pulled a blanket out of the hall closet. He stripped down to his boxers and stretched out on the couch. Pulling the blanket to his waist, he folded his arms behind his head. He stared at the ceiling, eyes wide-open.

She took a deep breath and floated toward him on the couch and asked, "What are you doing?"

He glanced over at her and swallowed hard. "I'm beginning to work something out. In the meantime, I'm going to sleep and you should, too. We have a big day ahead of us tomorrow."

She perched on the edge of the couch. Hovering over him, she said, "I don't want to sleep…alone. Last night I needed you. Tonight I want you."

Sitting up, he said, "I acted out of my own selfish desires the other day. I took advantage of the situation, of your vulnerability."

She tossed her head back. "I'm not vulnerable now, and it's my turn to be selfish. I may never see you again after tomorrow, and I want to feel your kisses again. I want you filling me up again. And again."

Emitting a low rumble from his throat, he reached out and pulled her face close to his. His mouth covered her lips and he kissed her hard, over and over. He kicked off the blanket and swung her on top of him. Her legs straddled his hips, and he thrust up against her hungrily. Then, holding her tightly against him, he got up and carried her to the bedroom.

This time their lovemaking was raw and powerful, as if they had to sear themselves onto each other's souls. Lila exulted in every moment, fearing she'd never experience his love again.

They remained motionless as they steadied their ragged breathing. Justin kissed her forehead, the tip of her nose and her bruised lips before rolling off the bed. When he left her side, an aching loss lanced her belly. How could she leave him?

He brought back a glass of water to share with her, and then they crawled under the covers.

Their hands began exploring. Their lips and mouths soon followed. Their desire, unquenched, rose unabated. And they made love again. And again.

Justin sank back against his pillow, his body heavy and sated. Lila curled on her side, her backside pressing against his hip, and stared out the window. His breathing deepened, slow and steady. She inched away from him. His hand fell from her shoulder. She sat up. He stirred. She remained still on the edge of the bed, holding her breath.

She pushed up from the bed, sweeping her clothes from the chair as she left the room. She eased the bedroom door closed and crept into the living room. Justin's cell phone sat next to his computer on the kitchen table. She picked it up and clicked through the electronic phonebook. Leo Caine.

She pressed the speed-dial button and waited.

The silky voice flowed over the line. "Taking it down to the wire, aren't you, Vidal?"

She whispered, "This is Lila Monroe. Tell me what to do."

The hateful voice chuckled. "I get it. Justin won't let you come and save your son? I was afraid of that."

"Just tell me where to go."

He gave her directions to a block of abandoned warehouses on the pier of Point Mar, warning her to come alone.

"Because if you don't, I'll kill your son."

She bit back a cry. "I'll be there. Alone."

Replacing Justin's phone, she glanced at the bedroom door. Still closed. She ached to go back into that room, kiss him, tell him goodbye.

She grabbed her bag and purse and slipped out the front door. She climbed into the Porsche, releasing the parking brake and cranking the steering wheel to the left. Grateful that Justin's house sat at the top of a hill, she dug in behind the car and pushed it forward. It started a slow roll down the street, and she ran along the side, jumping in at the bottom of the hill.

She started the engine and headed south.

Her throat ached with unshed tears as she left behind the man she loved. He'd finally opened up to her, let her in, and she'd betrayed him. Just like everyone else in his life.

Chapter Twelve

Darkness hung over San Diego like a gray blanket as Lila sped down to Point Mar. Her excitement over seeing Tyler pumped enough adrenaline through her system to keep her alert, even though she hadn't slept at all.

She lay with Justin's strong arms wrapped around her after they made love. Wide awake. Knowing she had to leave him. Spent and drained, he slept deeply, never suspecting her betrayal.

A sigh escaped her lips. He ravished her last night. There was no other word for it. His demanding kisses left her lips swollen. He took her completely, claiming every inch of her body as his own. And she offered it to him willingly. She felt his hands and lips on her body even now, her nerve endings tingling with his remembered touch.

Her senses recalled every nuance of his lovemaking as if experiencing it anew. His scent lingered with her, masculine, musky. The taste of herself on his mouth after he devoured her stained her lips. She swallowed a groan as the slow heat of desire kindled within her again.

She buzzed the window down, gulping the cool ocean air with its tangy flavor of salt and brine. The docks of Point Mar loomed ahead. Thinking of Tyler held captive on the dark pier, she shoved her foot down on the accelerator.

She swung into a parking space and stepped out of the car, the mist settling on her hair and eyelashes. Her sandals scuffed on the bumpy metal of the pier as she edged closer to a group of abandoned warehouses.

A buoy clanged, its lonesome sound echoing in the haze. The fog sucked her into its grasp, muffling her senses as she stumbled along the pier. She felt as if she was entering a different world, leaving the safety of Justin's embrace behind. As the water lapped against the stone buttresses of the pier, it sloshed beneath her feet, the only relief to the silence.

Approaching the huddled buildings, she peered into the hazy darkness. Was that movement? A door creaked open and she drew back. A waxy light spilled from the crack in the doorway. She held her breath, gripping the strap of her bag.

The door widened, and a figure hovered in the entrance, throwing a long shadow across her path. "Ms. Monroe?"

Clearing her throat, she answered, "Yes."

The man stepped forward, the light creating a dull shine on his bald pate. She expected a monster, but an ordinary man stood before her, indistinguishable in every way save his cleanly shaven head and dark goatee.

His pointed beard matched his pointed ears, and for a moment she felt as if she faced the devil. Not an ordinary man at all.

He gestured her into the warehouse. "I hope you came alone, Ms. Monroe, or…" He shrugged his shoulders, elegantly clad in a tailored shirt.

She assured him, "I'm alone."

His teeth gleamed in the darkness. "That's good. Don't be shy, come on in. I'm sure you're anxious to see your son."

She brushed past him into the warehouse, his stale cologne and sweat assaulting her nostrils. The strong smell of fish replaced his unpleasant odor, and she gagged thinking of Tyler spending the night in this place.

The man held out his hand. "I'm Leo Caine. You can call me Leo."

Lila ignored the hand and stated, "I can think of a lot of names to call you, and Leo isn't my first choice."

He chuckled. "I can see we're going to have an interesting journey to Mexico together."

"Where's my son?"

He swept the hand he still held in front of him to the side with a flourish. She almost expected smoke and the smell of sulfur to accompany the gesture. "Follow me."

She walked behind him into a small, cluttered room, which looked as if it had been used as an office for the warehouse. A young man sat cross-legged on the floor next to a sleeping bag. Tyler's fair hair stuck out of the top of the sleeping bag, and she rushed to him and crouched down.

He mumbled in his sleep as she brushed his long hair from his forehead. She ran her fingers along the back of his head and felt a hard lump.

She turned on Caine. "Why did your flunky hit him?"

Spreading his manicured hands, he sighed. "You should pity my...flunky." He nodded toward the man on the floor. "Your son sunk his teeth into Massoud's hand and kicked his shin. Massoud had to subdue him."

She snorted. "And the housekeeper? Did he have to subdue her, too?"

His small dark eyes opened wide. "I didn't hear about that one. We do what we have to, Ms. Monroe. Or may I call you Lila?"

Ignoring his request, she said, "And why do you have to betray your country, Mr. Caine?"

He twisted thin lips. "You've been spending too much time in the company of Lone Wolf, Lila. This is just a little business arrangement. Nothing more."

She scoffed, "A little business arrangement that's going to result in a horrific event, a family event, perhaps killing thousands of people?"

Shaking his head, he said, "Victoria revealed a lot more than I thought, but then she always did have a soft spot for Lone Wolf. Most women do—all that brooding angst."

Caine sounded envious, but Lila didn't want to talk about Justin, didn't want to hear about him. Guilt still twisted in her gut like a knotted rag. "Why are you doing this?"

He rubbed his hands together. "Money. Maybe that seems like a paltry motive to you since you have so much of it already."

More envy? The man thrived on it.

He laughed. "I don't know how Justin thought he could hide the former Mrs. Gareth Stone, cofounder of TouchStone. He must be slipping."

Her teeth sawed her bottom lip. She should've told Justin everything, should've trusted him. "I didn't reveal that part of my identity."

"Who are you, Ms. Monroe? Why were you with Chad in Mexico when he stumbled onto the tunnel?"

She took Tyler's hand and pressed it to her lips. "My car broke down, and Chad picked me up."

His dark eyes burned into her. "Oh, I see. You slept with him."

Justin had believed the same thing. She said between clenched teeth, "I did not."

He lifted one shoulder. "It's not for me to judge. Chad's attraction to the ladies and theirs to him served him well, even to the very end."

She didn't bother explaining that her attraction veered toward a different type of man—a sexy, mysterious man with a single-minded desire for justice. "I'm not even sure I remember where Chad died. And how do you know the tunnel is located there?"

"Victoria told me Justin brought you in to the HIA field office and took you straight to the navigation room. He wouldn't have been interested in the location of Chad's execution if it weren't meaningful. Lone Wolf's not the type to lay flowers at the sight of a fallen comrade."

Another man walked in the door, a pistol shoved in the waistband of his pants. He said something in Arabic to Leo, who answered in the same language and sent him back outside.

"Looks like you followed orders, Lila. No one on your trail yet."

She grimaced. "I told you, I came alone."

"That wasn't much of a dilemma for Justin, was it? Save one boy's life in exchange for giving up the location of that tunnel and saving thousands. I knew he wouldn't be too hot on the idea, but I knew you would be. You must've snuck away from him. How'd you manage that? Slip something in his drink?"

Her cheeks burned and tears pricked her eyes when she remembered how she'd coaxed Justin into having sex with her so she could slip away. Oh no, it was more than that. She'd wanted him, wanted his body next to hers. He'd been acting so damn chivalrous when she knew he wanted her, too.

She brushed her hand across her eyes. That all ended when she left him. Gesturing to Tyler, she asked, "How long has he been sleeping?"

Caine rolled his eyes. "Not long enough."

"What does that mean?" she said sharply.

"The kid never shuts up. He finally fell asleep about eleven o'clock. If you want to talk to him before we leave for Mexico, you better wake him up. We're going to hit the road soon."

"Will I have a chance to call my ex-husband to pick him up?"

He didn't answer. "Wake him up so we can get going. I have a feeling Vidal's going to try to beat us down there, but without you, he'll be lost."

Without him, I'm lost. The thought flashed across her mind, but she let it go just as she had to let him go.

Squeezing Tyler's shoulder, she leaned in and kissed his soft cheek. She whispered, "Tyler. Tyler."

His eyes flew open, and he stared at nothing for a moment. He blinked a few times, rolling onto his side.

Lila stroked his cheek. "It's Mom. I'm here."

He sat up, and then threw himself into her arms. He sobbed, "Mom."

Hugging him tightly, she said, "It's all right. I'm here now."

He sniffed and knuckled his eyes. "Mom, is it true you're going to Mexico with this guy? I heard him on the phone. He said he's taking you to Mexico."

She rubbed his back. "Just for a little while. Your dad's going to come get you, and I'll have him call Grams. She'll take you home."

His watery smile made her heart skip.

She ran her fingers over the bump on the back of his head. "How's your head?"

His fingers replaced hers. "It's okay. I figured out that the circumference of the bump is three centimeters. I used my fingernail to measure it 'cuz I know the length of my fingernail."

He wrinkled his nose. "Unless my fingernail's grown since I last measured it."

She ruffled his hair. "It's close enough."

Caine said something to Massoud, and he hopped to his feet. He slipped on some shoes and left the building.

Caine waved toward him. "I sent him to pick up some breakfast."

Even though her stomach rumbled, she didn't want to waste any more time. "I'm not hungry, and my son can eat when he gets to his father's home."

Caine turned away and said, "He's not going home right away."

Lila sprang to her feet. "What do you mean? I'm here. I'm going to Mexico with you to show you where

Chad died. That's our deal. I come with you, and you release my son."

He turned back, hunching his shoulders. "Not exactly, Lila. I told you your son would be safe once you showed me the tunnel. Not before. If I release him now, what guarantee do I have that you're going to take me to the right place?"

She took a step toward him, clenching her fists. "I'm giving you my word. Let him go now, and I'll take you to the tunnel."

Glancing down at her hands, he said, "Can't do that, Lila. Don't worry. Once you take me to the tunnel and leave Mexico, I'll call my man here to release your son. Then you can put this whole incident behind you."

She swallowed the bile that rose from her gut. Justin was right. Would this man even release her after she took him to the tunnel? How could he if he thought she'd rush straight to Justin? What about Tyler? What would happen to him once she left him here? Her blood iced in her veins. She couldn't leave him here.

Oh God, she needed Justin.

Tyler scrambled out of his sleeping bag. "Don't leave me here, Mom. I don't want to stay here without you."

She pulled him toward her, putting her arm around his shoulders. She pleaded with Caine. "Please, I'll tell you where Chad died. Then you can let us both go. Or keep us here together until you find the tunnel."

He tugged on his beard. "That won't work. I need you to help me find the tunnel, and I need your son as insurance you'll do it."

She stiffened her back, refusing to show weakness

in front of this man or in front of her son. She sat down on the sleeping bag, bringing Ty down with her. He snuggled against her side.

"All right. But if you hurt my son, I'll come after you myself. Or Justin Vidal will." Was that just bravado? Would Justin help her at all now?

He smiled. "If all goes well, we'll find the tunnel and I'll be on my way to some undisclosed island destination."

She narrowed her eyes. "You're the most despicable kind of traitor. You don't believe in any cause. You don't believe in anything but money. You have a rude awakening in store for you, Mr. Caine."

He waved his hands in front of him. "Oh, I know. Money doesn't buy everything."

"Don't you care what happens to your country? Your fellow citizens?"

"Don't be melodramatic, Lila. It's just one event in one city. Not that many people will be affected."

Her jaw dropped. She'd often been accused of being naive, but this man was oblivious. "You don't have to be directly involved for something like this to have an impact on you. It doesn't even have to be in this country. Terrorism affects all of us."

Clasping his hands behind his back, he said, "You're right. It affected me profoundly. After twenty years in a thankless job with the CIA, I got a call from the Department of Homeland Security, offering me a new position as sector chief for a field office of the newly created Homeland Intelligence Agency."

"That wasn't enough for you?"

He smirked. "You're accustomed to private industry. I assure you, the government doesn't pay nearly as well, especially for a man of my refined tastes. But I did learn about a few rich Saudis who support and finance Al Tariq. I figured they'd pay me handsomely for some inside information. And they do."

Lila's stomach turned. He'd solicited them.

He snapped his fingers. "Enough of politics. This is my last job for Al Tariq. I'm going to officially retire after this."

Lila had a feeling Justin would never allow that. Had she given him enough information to find the tunnel on his own? Was there a possibility he would be there when she arrived with Leo? Then what? If the men holding Tyler didn't hear from Leo, did he have orders to kill? She clamped her teeth together to keep them from chattering. She had to reach Justin somehow.

The man, Massoud, returned with bags of fast-food breakfasts. He handed her two bags, and she realized she was starving. She'd hardly eaten a bite since Gareth's call announcing Ty's kidnapping.

She withdrew a breakfast burrito out of the bag and handed it to Tyler. He shook his head, but she leaned in and whispered in his ear, "You need your strength."

Leo barked out, "Stop whispering over there, or I'll separate you."

Tyler gazed up at her, and she winked. He took the burrito and wolfed it down in three bites. She ate hers, too, and drank the hot coffee from the foam cup.

Tyler asked out loud, "Who's Justin Vidal?"

Lila answered, "He's an agent who works for the same organization as this man, but he—"

Caine shouted, "Shut up. You don't need to know anything, kid. Just eat your breakfast."

Tyler glanced up at Lila from beneath his long lashes, and she nodded once. Was it enough to convey to him that Justin was a man he could trust?

Tyler asked for another burrito, and the quiet young man handed him a bag. Lila studied his face. Could he help? He scowled at her, and she dropped her eyes.

Seeing the look, Tyler spoke up, "I had a lot of fun at Dad's house this time."

Lila jerked her head up. Tyler rarely had fun at Gareth's house. She swallowed as Caine watched them. "Did you? What did you do?"

Munching his burrito, he said, "Played video games all day. Dad bought me a new one. Can I play it at Grams's? It's all about hunting down terrorists."

Leo chuckled while the young man in the corner glared at Tyler, and he glared back.

Tyler liked video games but hated being stuck indoors all day playing them. What was he driving at?

She feigned absentmindedness. "That's nice. As long as there's not too much violence."

Her son choked. "Mom, it's about hunting down terrorists. Of course there's violence."

She sighed. "I don't know why your father buys you inappropriate games."

He gulped his milk. "I bet you're not going to let me keep my cell phone, either."

Her head buzzed as she kept her voice steady. "Cell phone? Your father bought you a cell phone?"

Frowning, he said, "Yeah, but Liz took it away from me. She said they'd check with you first before getting me service for it."

That wasn't true. She remembered Graciela telling

them that Tyler was playing with his new cell phone when Leo's men abducted him.

Her heart raced, and she licked her lips. "Well, I'm certainly not going to allow that, Ty. You're too young."

He crumpled up a bag. "I thought you'd say that."

Leaning over her, he tossed the bag at Massoud. While he hit out at it and Leo turned, Tyler tapped the pocket of his shorts. Lila exhaled. Tyler had his cell phone in his pocket. Somehow she had to give him Justin's number.

Leo laughed. "These two are going to spend a couple of long days together. Too bad we don't have video games in the warehouse. They could hunt terrorists together."

Lila's brain whirred. Even if Ty could get Justin on the phone, he'd have to tell him where he was. Did Tyler even know where he was? "I didn't realize the pier at Point Mar had so many abandoned warehouses."

Ty blinked his eyes twice.

Caine looked up, his brow furrowed. His eyes shifted from Lila to Tyler before he answered. "It has a few."

He gestured to the empty bags littering the sleeping bag. "Are you finished eating? We have to get going. The sun's already up."

Lila glanced out the office door and peered up at the skylights in the warehouse. Was Justin awake yet? Did he realize what she'd done?

JUSTIN ROLLED onto his back. His brain fogged over as if he'd drunk too much wine. Sweet wine. His loins stirred. He turned to reach for Lila, but his searching hands met cold sheets.

He ran his tongue along his parched lips. The taste

of her feminine essence lingered there, and he savored it again.

"Lila?" He strained his ears to catch the breakfast sounds from the kitchen. Silence. He stared at the closed bedroom door. Unaccountably, his chest tightened.

Rising from the bed, he searched the floor for his boxers and shrugged. Not like she hadn't seen it all last night. And the night before.

Walking toward the door, he yelled, "I figured it out on the couch last night before you seduced me. How I'm going to get Tyler back."

He stepped into the small living room from where he could see the kitchen.

Empty.

He jerked his head toward the front door where she placed her bag last night.

Gone.

He strode to the window, pulling the blinds back. He stared at the vacant space where he parked the Porsche last night after dinner.

His stomach lurched.

Clenching his jaw so tightly his teeth crunched together, he stalked to the kitchen table. He grabbed his cell phone and hit the redial button. Leo's number flashed on the display before the call went through. It rang, but Leo didn't pick it up. He didn't need to.

Spinning around, he smashed his fist into the wall.

Once she led Leo to the tunnel, he'd kill her. And her son? He might let him go, but not before Lila gave him what he wanted.

He should've seen it. She'd acquiesced way too

quickly. She'd been willing to give Leo anything to see her son, and his lust had blinded him to that fact.

And her lust? Was it all for show? She'd used him. Distracted him.

He didn't even regret it. He regretted that her ploy worked, which put her right into Leo's clutches, but he didn't regret their passion. That was real. At least it was for him.

He didn't have the luxury of time to feel sorry for himself, or even angry at her. She did what she had to do. She didn't trust him, but how could he blame her for that?

He showered and dressed, reviewing his conversations with Victoria in his head. Had she mentioned anything about Leo having a secret hideaway? Had Leo himself hinted at his location over the phone?

After pacing the floor, he slumped in a chair at the kitchen table. He had no idea where Leo was or where he was keeping the boy.

His cell phone rang, and his hand shot out to grab it. "Vidal."

"Justin, this is Molina."

"Molina, where the hell are you?"

Molina coughed. "Dusty little Mexican village— Loma Vista. Thought that's where I'm supposed to be."

Justin expelled a long breath. "You made it. What happened in Costa Rica?"

"Haven't figured that out yet. Either someone scammed me to get me out of Mexico City and away from Chad, or my informant had some real information. Chad's dead and my informant's missing."

"Brooke said your informant had something on someone high up in the agency?"

"Yeah, but that could've been a scramble."

Justin said, "No, your informant had some real information for you."

Molina drew in a sharp breath. "What are you telling me?"

"It's Leo."

"Do you have proof?"

Justin told him about Prasad and Victoria and about how Lila was identified through her fingerprints at the compound. "I don't have anything that HIA headquarters is interested in yet, but he kidnapped the witness's son and he's forcing her to go with him to Mexico."

Molina swore. "Leo a traitor? Must be money."

Justin asked, "Do you know something I don't?"

Molina grunted. "Gambling and women. I guess Leo wasn't all that truthful on that part of the HIA application."

"Stay where you are. I'm coming down to Loma Vista."

"Do you have any idea where this tunnel is? This seems a little far from the border to be digging tunnels. That's one long walk underground, although the last one the Border Patrol discovered had lighting, drainage and a paved walkway. Next thing you know, they'll be building a hotel underground."

Justin chewed on the side of his thumb before replying. "I thought of that, but we have to save this witness. I'm afraid Leo's going to kill her once she leads him to the tunnel."

"You're probably right. What about her son?"

"I don't have a clue where Leo's holding him, but he'll keep him until Lila takes him to the tunnel."

"I'll stay right here and wait for you, and if I see that young fool Prasad running around, I'll rope him in."

Justin ended the call more hopeful than he'd been in a long time. He could count on Molina and possibly Prasad. Between the three of them, they'd find Leo and Lila. They had to.

LILA GLANCED at Leo as he finished his coffee. Time ticked away. Somehow she needed to give Tyler Justin's phone number. Thank God she memorized it. The rest she'd have to leave up to him. And Justin.

Because of Tyler's love for numbers, they did a lot of math puzzles and games. Could she just tell him the numbers? Surely Leo would understand what she was doing. Then what? She shivered.

Leo hoisted himself off the straight-backed chair and looked her way. "Are you ready?"

She stalled. "Are we going alone?"

"I can't take either of these two with me. Too risky getting them back and forth across the border. But Al Tariq has several men in Mexico ready to do my bidding. Once you lead me to the tunnel, I call them in."

Lila dragged in a breath. "What's going to happen to my son?"

"I'll leave him here with Massoud and Raheed. Once you show me the tunnel and leave Mexico, I'll call them here and tell them to release him."

She pressed. "Release him where? He's only ten years old."

"Oh, for God's sake, they can take him to a phone booth and he can call his father."

Lila's heart raced. Should she give Tyler Justin's

phone number pretending it's Gareth's? No, Caine might recognize it as Justin's number. She screamed in her head. She needed time.

Leo ordered, "Let's go."

She rose from the floor, and Tyler immediately started yelling and crying. "Don't go. Don't go. I don't want to stay here by myself. I want to go home and see my best friend."

Lila gasped. Tyler never threw tantrums, even as a two-year-old. She looked down at him pounding his fists on the floor and kicking his legs, and he turned his head sideways and winked at her.

Crouching down, she soothed, "It's all right, Tyler. I'll be back soon."

He thrashed his head from side to side, just like his best friend's little brother. Her hand flew to her mouth. His friend's mom gave the little brother a phrase to repeat over and over, which seemed to calm him down. Tyler told her about it just two months ago. Nowhere near as quick as her son, Lila began mouthing words and counting on her fingers, each word containing the number of letters corresponding to the numbers in Justin's phone number.

She blurted out, "The sun is sinking fast, wet suits required. The sun is sinking fast, wet suits required."

Caine jerked around and stared at her. "What are you saying?"

By this time, Tyler began repeating the phrase. "The sun is sinking fast, wet suits required."

Holding up her hands, she said, "When my son gets very upset, I give him a phrase to repeat over and over. It seems to calm him down."

She added, "The faster he calms down, the faster we can be on our way."

Caine shook his head but didn't object. Justin's phone number ran through her brain. The sun is sinking fast, wet suits required. Did he get it? One look at Tyler's face, his mouth mumbling the nonsensical words over and over, told her he did. Now he had to somehow make that call. And Justin had to still care enough to respond.

Caine studied them as they said goodbye, but Lila wasn't acting now. Tears coursed down her face as she left her little boy behind. Not even her love was strong enough to protect him, and not one good-luck ritual or incantation existed to change that.

Chapter Thirteen

Justin hunched over the kitchen table. He shoved the map of Mexico aside and put his head in his hands. God, why didn't Lila trust him? He could've saved her son from Leo. Were they on their way to Mexico now? The thought made his stomach clench, and he grabbed the map again and smoothed it out on the table.

Biting the inside of his cheek, he circled the area around Loma Vista, aptly named, as it sat at the base of the foothills. Tapping the map with his pencil, he frowned. He came back to the same problem that nagged him before. It just didn't make sense. Why would the coyotes, terrorists or anyone else be interested in a tunnel so far from the border? It could be to escape the notice of the Border Patrol, but it would cover almost one hundred miles. The effort involved in constructing such a tunnel would be immense, not to mention the fortitude needed to traverse it.

"El túnel está aquí." Chad's last words echoed in his brain. Did Lila misunderstand? He never even asked her how fluently she spoke Spanish. Most native Californians, with their smattering of Spanish,

could understand that phrase easily. But nonfluent speakers often had difficulty distinguishing words spoken so rapidly they ran together. Chad spoke Spanish like a native.

He wrote the words down on a piece of paper, putting it next to the map. Looking back and forth between the map and the paper, an idea began to crystallize. Tracking the pencil along the map, he ticked off points along the border.

He sucked in his breath and slapped the table. "That's it."

His cell phone rang, and he pounced on it, checking the display. An unknown number. It rang once more.

"Vidal."

A retching noise scratched over the line, and he gripped the phone until it almost popped out of his sweaty palms. Lila?

Before he could open his mouth to speak, he heard a voice. "Shh, hold on."

A child's voice.

More muffled noises and voices. Running water.

He waited.

Then quite clearly, "How much longer are you going to keep me in this abandoned warehouse in Point Mar?"

A breath hissed between Justin's teeth. Leo had them in Point Mar. Still, he waited and Lila's bright son rewarded him. "Those skylights are pretty cool."

Justin heard a man's voice respond and then nothing. But it was enough. After what he'd just discovered on the map, it had to be enough. Leo would kill Lila for sure.

Justin tossed his gear in the back of his truck and took off for Mexico with a stopover in Point Mar.

He parked the truck behind a tackle-and-bait shop, concealing it from the pier. He pulled a black knit cap over his head and shrugged into a windbreaker against the cool mist insinuating itself around him.

A few cars sat in the pier parking lot. Justin caught his breath. The black Porsche looked out of place next to the trucks and vans.

After buying a fishing pole and tackle box, he pulled up the collar of his windbreaker and hunched his shoulders as he walked onto the pier, joining several other early-morning fishermen.

Circling the pier once, he noted that most of the abandoned warehouses huddled on the southwest corner away from the fishing boats. Two of those warehouses had skylights. He watched. A man with dark, longish hair paced back and forth on the side of one of those warehouses. The lookout.

Dropping his fishing gear, Justin started out on the other side of the warehouse, flattening his body along the side of the building as he crept toward the man on sentry duty. He waited until the man spun around with his back to him.

Justin crouched and swiftly covered the distance between them. Before the lookout became aware of company, Justin had him around the throat, choking off a startled cry. He moved his fingers to the sides of the man's neck and squeezed. He slumped, and Justin dragged him to the warehouse doorway.

He tried the knob. Locked. He'd already discovered this was the only door to the warehouse besides the large track doors. The building had no windows except the skylights.

He banged on the warehouse door and called out in Arabic, "Let me in."

After a few moments, a voice called back from the other side in Arabic, "Who is it? What do you want?"

Justin recognized the dialect and answered with the same in a guttural voice. "Someone's coming. Let me in."

The door cracked open. Justin barreled through it, knocking the man to the side. The man raised a gun. Justin straightened up. He kicked the man's hand toward the ceiling, sending the bullet smashing into the skylight. Glass rained down on them as the man took aim again. Justin lunged at his legs, bringing him down hard. The gun skittered away as the man's head cracked against the glass-littered floor.

Justin checked the pulse in his throat. His breath rattled in his chest and blood seeped out of the corner of his mouth and one ear. He withdrew a length of rope from his jacket and tied the man's wrists and ankles. Then he dragged the other man, still unconscious, into the warehouse and bound him in a similar fashion.

Just as he finished tying the last knot, he heard a voice behind him. "You better be Justin Vidal."

He spun around. A boy lounged in the doorway of an office, his arms folded across his chest, curly blond hair tumbling into his eyes.

Justin nodded once and put a finger to his lips. He checked the knots, stood up and whispered, "Are you alone?"

The boy nodded his head, his gaze taking in the two bound and gagged men on the floor. He swept his hair back from his face, and Justin took a step back from those clear blue eyes so much like Lila's.

He asked, "Are you Tyler?"

The boy answered, "Yeah. I'm Tyler Stone."

Justin blew out a long breath. "Where's your mom?"

Tyler threw a gangly arm toward the door. "She left with the bald guy. They went to Mexico."

Justin swore softly.

Tyler grinned. "I don't think my mom would want you to say words like that in front of me, but I don't mind."

Narrowing his eyes, Justin asked, "How'd you get my number? How'd you know to call me?"

Heaving himself off the doorjamb, Tyler said, "My mom basically told me to call you. I guess she thought you could help us out."

He explained the game they'd played so Lila could give him Justin's number without Leo being aware of it. "Then after the bald guy took Mom, I faked being sick. While I pretended to hurl in the bathroom, I called you."

Justin's throat tightened. So she did trust him. Better late than never. He looked down into her son's eyes. Not much trust there.

The boy's eyes, so similar in color and shape to Lila's, held a different quality. Wariness. Skepticism. Could someone this young be cynical already? He snorted to himself. Who was he to ask a question like that? Although Tyler's childhood beat out his by a long shot, divorce always took a toll on kids, and if his first impression of Gareth Stone was correct, the man wouldn't be winning any father-of-the-year awards.

Justin's face relaxed, and he asked, "Are you okay? Did they hurt you?"

Tyler rubbed the back of his head. "I'm okay. I just have a huge lump on my head."

Justin ran his fingers through Tyler's curly, sun-bleached hair and prodded the bump on his head.

Tyler jerked his head away. "Ouch. You couldn't just take my word for it?"

Justin mumbled, "Sorry." Kate's three kids were younger than Tyler, toddlers and babies. He hadn't carried on an actual conversation with a kid in a long time.

Shoving his hands into the pockets of his shorts, Tyler asked, "Are you really a spy?" His eyes glimmered with interest and curiosity.

"Sort of. How long ago did your mom and the bald guy leave?"

Tyler screwed up his eyes. "Probably less than an hour ago. I don't know. How long did it take you to get here after I called you?"

Checking his watch, Justin said, "About forty-five minutes."

Tyler looked up at the broken skylight. "She left about fifty minutes ago then. Are we going to follow them?"

Justin's eyebrows shot up. "We?"

The boy's blue eyes glittered as he folded his arms across his skinny chest again. "If you think I'm going to wait around here with these two guys, you're crazy."

Justin clenched his jaw. Stubborn. "I'll drop you off at your father's house, or I'll wait here with you while I call in some people to take care of this." He jerked a thumb at the two men on the floor. HIA headquarters would have to move in now.

Tyler shook his head from side to side. "We have to

get my mom as soon as possible. That guy's going to hurt her once she shows him the tunnel, isn't he?"

Justin avoided the question. "How much do you know about what's going on?"

"Enough. Enough to know Leo's going to hurt my mom. She may not think so."

Tyler scuffed at the smooth warehouse floor with the toe of his shoe, and then raised his eyes to Justin's. "My mom always thinks everything's going to be okay, but sometimes it's not."

Tyler's lip quivered, and Justin busied himself by checking on the two trussed-up men. He didn't know much about kids, but he did know a boy Tyler's age didn't want to be caught crying.

Tyler's voice steadied. "We have to follow them right now. And I'm going with you."

Damn, the boy was right. It was too late to have Leo and Lila stopped at the border, even if he knew what kind of car Leo was driving. Leo would be carrying a fake passport, too. He had to get on their trail as soon as possible.

He could leave Tyler in Loma Vista, or maybe if Prasad was down there, he could leave him with Prasad. They didn't have time to wait around for the HIA or to stop off at Gareth Stone's house.

Gripping Tyler's shoulders, he looked into his face. "Listen to me. I'm taking you with me, but you have to do everything I tell you to do. Understand?"

He shrugged Justin's hands off his shoulders. "Yeah, I get it." Then he slumped. "I can't go."

Justin asked, "Why not?"

"I don't have my passport or birth certificate. Mom

took me down there last year, and she brought my birth certificate along."

Smart kid. "Don't worry about that."

Eyeing him suspiciously, Tyler said, "Are you going to sneak me into Mexico illegally?"

Justin sighed. Not at all like Lila. "Not illegally, but I can get you through. You have anything you want to bring with you? I'm going to make a few phone calls."

While Tyler returned to the small office, Justin phoned HIA headquarters in D.C. and explained the situation. Headquarters agreed to send a couple of agents to the warehouse to pick up and question the two men.

He placed his next call to Gareth Stone's house. Graciela answered the phone. Stone was already at the office. Working. Justin filed away that information. Stone would have a hard time justifying this in a custody hearing.

He told Graciela that Tyler was safe, and she sobbed her relief into the phone. At least one member of that household cared enough to wait by the phone.

He felt Tyler's presence at his shoulder and turned. "I called your father to let him know you're safe."

Those blue eyes burned into his. "That wasn't my father on the phone."

Justin didn't look away, even though he wanted to. "Your father was already at work. I spoke to Graciela."

Tyler's eyes flickered. "We better go."

The pier bustled with activity. Fishing boats headed out to sea. Fishermen huddled in groups along the pier's edge trading stories, oblivious to the violence in the abandoned warehouse on the far side.

One thought pounded in Justin's head, keeping pace with his footsteps ringing across the pier. *I hope I'm not too late. I hope I'm not too late.*

Tyler scampered beside him to keep up but didn't seem to mind. His clear child's voice gave substance to Justin's fear. "I hope we're not too late."

Justin reached back and ruffled the boy's hair. "Don't worry. We'll get there in time."

Tyler stopped and put his hands up. "Don't touch the hair."

Justin halted next to him, raising his eyebrows.

A slow pink stain rose to Tyler's cheeks, and he looked down. "I'm sorry. My mom says I'm rude sometimes. It's just that I don't like people touching me. Or feeling sorry for me…except my mom."

Justin swallowed hard. He knew the feeling. "No problem."

As they walked off the pier and into the parking lot, an old fisherman with hooks swinging from his hat gave them a toothless smile. "Did you enjoy a morning's fishing with your dad?"

Without blinking an eye or missing a step, Tyler answered, "Yeah, I did."

LILA LEANED FORWARD and winked at the Border Patrol agent. She couldn't see his eyes masked behind his dark sunglasses, but they obviously weren't trained on her. He handed their passports back to Leo and said, "Enjoy your day in Mexico."

Lila collapsed back in her seat. Not likely.

Leo chuckled. "Nice try, Lila. You wouldn't really want to succeed anyway. I still have your son."

As they left the hubbub of Tijuana, she stared out the window at the brown foothills. "This could be a wild-goose chase for all you know. All I can show you is the spot where Chad died. Where he was murdered. Where you had him murdered."

Leo clucked his tongue. "Perhaps. But there must be something there. Some clue. Otherwise, Justin Vidal wouldn't be so interested in you."

She winced.

He noticed. He clicked his tongue and shook his head. "It's like that, is it? Don't flatter yourself, honey. Lone Wolf wouldn't have kept you with him unless you were instrumental in achieving his goal. And his goal right now is to beat me to the tunnel and destroy it before Al Tariq can send its men and supplies through for the attack."

Lila squeezed her eyes closed. Leo probably spoke the truth. He knew the man better than she did. A physical ache throbbed in her belly, and she folded her arms over her stomach, hugging herself. A tear threatened to escape the corner of her eye, so she squeezed everything tighter.

Would Justin rescue Tyler after her abandonment? Was Tyler even able to reach him? She clamped down harder, grinding her teeth together. What would the men do to Tyler if they caught him trying to make a call?

Her eyes slid to Leo's cell phone tucked in the pocket of his polo shirt. Surely Massoud would call Leo if Tyler tried something. She forced air out of her mouth and drew a ragged breath back in.

Leo pulled the car over to the side of the road. He dropped a map in Lila's lap and said, "Where to?"

Her hands trembled as she unfolded the map and laid it out in front of her. She'd already located the spot once in the navigation room at the HIA compound. Could she do it again? She traced her finger down from the border and veered off the main road. The squiggly brown lines indicated the foothills, and she squinted at the small print at their base. Loma Vista.

She poked at the map. "There."

Leo leaned across her, and she turned her head away from his stench…new sweat layered upon stale sweat.

His head jerked up. "Impossible."

She looked into his dark eyes, flat and opaque with anger. His ears seemed even more pointed than before.

Speaking around the lump in her throat, she said, "It wasn't exactly in Loma Vista. It was about an hour's drive south of there. I can't find the location on the map, but once we drive down to Loma Vista, I think I can find it from there."

He drove his fist into the map, punching her thigh in the process. She flattened herself against the door.

"Impossible."

"What do you mean?"

Crumpling the map in one hand, he growled, "I mean, that's too far from the border for a tunnel. You're lying."

She stared down at the fist balled around the map, mesmerized by the black hair scattered across the back of his hand. Justin had voiced the same concern. The site of Chad's death lay too far from the border to start digging a tunnel.

But she remembered his words clearly. "The tunnel is here." Or did she? She hadn't recalled those words when she first gave Justin an account of the scene. She remembered only after he told her Chad and he had been searching for a tunnel.

She took a great shuddering breath and licked her lips before beginning. "I told you before. I never saw any tunnel. All I can show you is where he died."

Leo grunted and returned his fist to his own lap. "You better not be lying to me. Massoud and Raheed still have your son. If I don't find something, some clue, some hint at the spot where Chad died, you'll die in the same place."

Lila powered down the window and gulped the dusty air as Leo churned the car back onto the road. Had Chad stopped south of Loma Vista just to hook up with the man who was going to show him the tunnel? The man who wound up dead? Maybe the guy had planned to take him to the tunnel from Loma Vista. Had Chad's last words been a trick?

The grit swirling in the air clung to her lip balm, and she wiped her hand across her mouth, depositing a few grains of dirt on her tongue. Perhaps she should make this suggestion to Leo. He couldn't blame her that Chad didn't die where the tunnel was located.

She stole a glance at his profile. *El diablo.* His pointed beard jutted forward, and even his eyebrows seemed to tilt upward. Oh, no, she couldn't tell him now. Maybe later. Maybe once they got to that clearing…with Justin waiting for them.

They careened down the main highway until Leo turned off toward the smaller road that snaked inland, away from the coast and toward the low-lying hills.

Lila pointed to the sign announcing Loma Vista in another two miles.

Leo checked his watch. "Took you almost an hour to get here after Chad was murdered?"

Lila nodded. "I was going pretty fast though."

She raised her hand as Leo sped past the turnoff to Loma Vista. "That was it. I stopped there for gas and food."

Leo shrugged. "We're not doing a reenactment here. I just want to get to the spot."

Lila craned her neck, looking back toward Loma Vista, her eyes glued to the scrubby, desolate landscape. Empty.

How was Justin ever going to find her now?

JUST BEFORE Justin hit the border, Molina called with the news that Prasad had joined him in Loma Vista. Damn kid. But at least one problem solved itself.

Once through the border stop, Justin dragged the back of his hand across his damp brow. Another problem solved. He felt Tyler's question needling the side of his face like pinpricks before he even spoke one word.

As they drove away from the border into Mexico, Tyler asked, "What was that piece of paper you showed him?"

Justin concentrated on the road in front of him, already awakening to the sounds of traffic. The kid had been issuing a flow of nonstop questions ever since they peeled out of San Diego.

"A birth certificate."

"Mine?"

Justin nodded.

Tyler tried again. "I know you don't have my birth certificate, so whose was it?"

Justin shrugged. "Just a spare."

Wrinkling his nose, Tyler asked, "Do you always keep spare birth certificates in your car?"

Justin glanced at him. The kid was dogged. You had to give him that. He gestured to the black bag on the floor of the truck. "Birth certificates, passports, drivers' licenses."

Tyler scooped up the bag and began rummaging through it, pulling out passports and other forms of identification. "Wow, you weren't kidding."

Justin dipped his head.

Tyler dropped the bag back on the floor. "Can you tell me what you do?"

"No."

"How'd my mom get involved?"

"She just tried to help someone out."

Tyler sighed. "Yeah, she does that a lot."

Justin said more sharply than he intended, "That's a good thing."

Tyler's searching gaze scorched his profile. The kid was worse than his mother—asking probing questions, demanding responses, trying to read his mind. Between the two of them he'd never felt so…alive.

Tyler butt into his thoughts again. "My dad doesn't think so."

Blinking his eyes, Justin said, "What?"

"My dad doesn't think it's a good thing when my mom tries to help people. Says she's a sap."

Justin ground his teeth together and gripped the steering wheel. He glanced at Tyler, whose eyes narrowed into a remarkably adult look. Was he waiting for him to defend his mother or confirm his father's words? He wasn't about to get in the middle of that.

Justin forced his face to relax and shrugged. "You have to decide for yourself."

Tyler drew back, his eyes widening. He watched Justin for another moment as if expecting him to withdraw his statement and tell him what to think.

He settled back in his seat and sighed. "I think my mom's great."

Justin grinned at him. "So do I."

Pulling his map from the door slot, Justin said, "We're headed for a little town called Loma Vista. Do you think you can find it on the map? I circled it."

Tyler unfolded the map and laid it flat on his lap. "I see it. Have we left Tijuana yet?"

"Just."

"How many miles per hour are you driving?"

Justin raised his brows. "About forty."

Tyler closed his eyes, and then they flew open. "We'll be there in about forty minutes."

Justin whistled. "That's pretty good. Your mom told me you were a math genius."

Tyler hunched a shoulder and reddened to the roots of his blond hair. "Not really. I just like numbers. I can calculate all the stats for the Padres. It helps when I'm surfing, too." He hesitated. "Do you surf?"

"I used to. Don't have a lot of time for it now."

Tyler expelled a long breath. "Long board?"

"Yeah. Some of the best long-board surfing I've done was off the coast of Indonesia."

Tyler's eyes brightened as he fired a series of questions at him about surfing. They passed the time in easy conversation until Justin saw the turnoff for Loma Vista.

His thoughts turned to Lila…alone after witnessing a murder and then finding a dead body in the car. He shook his head. How had she managed to keep it together?

His eyes tracked over the boy next to him. Kidnapped. His mother taken from that abandoned warehouse. And here he was chattering about surfing. They were made of strong stuff.

As he pulled up in front of the roadside café, Molina and Prasad didn't even rise from the porch. They looked like permanent fixtures already.

Justin swore when he saw Prasad's fingers wrapped around the long neck of a beer bottle. Great. As far as he knew, Prasad never took a drink in his life. Now wasn't the time to start.

He eased out of the car and gestured toward Prasad as he asked Molina, "Are you corrupting his morals?"

Prasad jumped up from his seat, and Molina laughed. "Somebody's gotta do it."

Prasad stammered, "I—it's just one. Danny thought I needed to relax."

Molina strolled down the steps and grasped Justin's hand. "What the hell took you so long?"

Justin beckoned to Tyler still waiting in the car. "Slight detour."

As Tyler climbed out of the truck, Prasad gasped and Danny's mouth dropped open. "The witness's son?"

"Long story." He wasn't about to go into how a ten-year-old boy manipulated him.

Tyler gestured toward the two men. "Are these the good guys?"

Justin snorted. "Hard to believe, I know."

Both Danny and Prasad shook Tyler's hand and introduced themselves.

Danny asked, "How old are you? Eleven? I have a boy your age."

Tyler said, "Almost. Do you surf, too?"

Danny shook his head. "Takes way too much energy."

Turning toward Justin, Danny asked, "What's the plan? We didn't see Leo come this way, but then we didn't move from this porch."

Justin tapped his head. "I have Lila's directions in here. We're going to the place where Al Tariq executed Chad."

Danny tossed his empty bottle in the trash can. "Let's go. I have some weapons and explosives in my car. You lead me to that tunnel and I'll blow it to kingdom come."

Typical Danny—always ready for action. He shook his head. "Can't do that right now, Danny."

Danny crossed his arms over his pumped-up chest. "Why not? Thought that's why we were all gathered in this godforsaken place."

Justin squinted at the clump of trees in the distance marking the end of the desert and the beginning of the jungle.

He spit into the dirt. "Can't do it because the tunnel's not here."

Chapter Fourteen

"The tunnel's not here." Leo thrashed around the under-brush with a stick, jabbing fruitlessly at the thickly car-peted ground.

Lila gulped at the wisps of sea breeze filtering through the trees. Now. She had to tell Leo her theory now.

She cleared her throat. "I was thinking before. Maybe Chad just said 'The tunnel is here' to throw off the men who were threatening him. Maybe he tried to trick them."

The hand materialized out of nowhere, smacking across her left cheek. Staggering back, she threw her arms out to maintain her balance. Tears flooded her eyes from the sting of the blow, and her ear buzzed.

She looked into Leo's dull orbs, slightly protruding from their sockets, and raised her hands to ward off the fury emanating from them.

He spoke through his teeth, barely moving his lips. "Do you mean to tell me Chad said 'The tunnel is here' before he died?"

Her fingertips traced the scorching handprint on her face. She swallowed the knot in her throat that threat-ened to explode in a burst of rage. He still had Tyler.

She whispered, "Yes."

Leo twisted the point of his beard and murmured, "Maybe he did try to trick them."

Lila sagged against the trunk of a twisted tree. Her tongue flicked over her lips, tasting the salty blood. Fear left its tracks up and down her spine, cinching the back of her neck. The tunnel wasn't here.

Justin had always had his doubts. Had he figured it out? And if he had figured it out, was he on his way to find the real location of the tunnel?

Something more than terror had her in its grip now. An acute sorrow claimed her belly, making her double over. Once again, she'd trusted unwisely and it was going to cost her her life. Worse. Tyler's life.

Justin tried to warn her off. Tried to tell her he was a loner not worth reclaiming. She should've believed him. Why did she think she could be the one to save him? The one to bring happiness and meaning into his empty life?

His lovemaking had been all about need. His physical needs. She couldn't deny the sensual connection between them. But that's all it was. An outlet. In the end, she didn't mean any more to him than Chad did. A means to an end. And Tyler meant even less.

She was here alone with *el diablo* in this clearing. Where it all started. He had Tyler, and he considered her worthless now. It would all end for her here, just as it had for Chad. There was no one to save her. No one to save Tyler.

DANNY AND PRASAD studied the map Justin laid out for them. Danny clapped Justin on the back. "Very clever of you. Now, let's get moving. We'll head out there our-selves and call in the Border Patrol to meet us."

Justin shook his head. "Not so fast. Al Tariq is ready to move. I think we should let them."

Danny scratched the dark stubble of his beard. "Go on."

Justin replied, "If we destroy the tunnel now and Leo knows about it, Al Tariq will slip away. Maybe they'll find another way in."

Tyler, his eyes bright with interest, walked up to the table. "I get it. Lead the terrorists to the tunnel and then catch them there."

Justin said, "That's it. I think I just found your re-placement, Molina."

Danny responded with a gesture, and then glanced at Tyler. "Sorry, kid."

Tyler grinned while Justin said, "Don't mind him. He told me crude language and gestures don't bother him at all. Just don't do it in front of his mother."

Prasad asked, "Okay, but how are we going to let Leo know about the true location of the tunnel? We can't just call and tell him."

Justin said, "Don't forget. He still has Lila."

He couldn't forget that if he tried. He and Tyler had made good time, but Leo and Lila were probably al-ready at the clearing. It wouldn't take Leo long to figure out that the tunnel didn't exist where Chad had died. Would he also understand Lila didn't lead him there as some kind of trick? His heart galloped in his chest, fueled by urgency and fear.

He continued, "I'll offer to tell him the location of the tunnel in exchange for Lila."

Turning to Tyler, he said, "You'll have to stay out of

sight, so he thinks he still has you as a bargaining chip. He may be more willing to give up your mom if he thinks he still has you. Prasad, you have to stay here with Tyler."

Prasad started to open his mouth, and Justin held up his hand. "I don't want to hear it. You're not supposed to be here anyway."

Danny asked, "You want me to come with you?"

Justin said, "No. I don't want Leo to know you're here, either. It's better if he thinks I'm on my own. Call the Border Patrol and HIA headquarters. Let them know what the plan is. They'll have to stake out the area and be ready to move when Al Tariq arrives."

Danny studied him. "You know he'll kill you if he can."

Shrugging, Justin said, "I just have to make sure he can't."

For his sake, as well as Lila's.

As Justin gave his final instructions, Tyler stepped forward, his eyes downcast. "Mr. Vidal? Please save my mom."

Justin's throat tightened as he started to reach forward and then dropped his hand. "I plan to."

THIRTY-FIVE MINUTES LATER, Justin's truck approached a grove of palmetto and boojum trees. He glanced up and down the road. No other trees bunched together like this. Then he saw the dirty white sedan tucked away up the access road.

He withdrew his gun and crept forward. The murmur of voices floated on the air, and he followed them to their source. Crouching down, he peered between two bushes into a small clearing. Leo and Lila stood next to each other near a twisted tree. In the next moment, Leo slapped Lila's face.

A low growl rumbled in Justin's throat. Instinctively, he raised his weapon, gripping it tightly, a white finger poised on the trigger.

Lila staggered back against the tree, her hand raised to her cheek. Justin could kill Leo for that alone. He drew in short, calming breaths and waited. There was more at stake here.

Leo took a few steps away from Lila. *That's it. Keep on moving.*

Stroking his beard, Leo looked down. His lips moved, but Justin couldn't hear his words. He sidled along the edge of the clearing until he was about five feet from Lila.

Justin hissed, and Lila swung her head around. Keeping an eye on Leo, Justin beckoned Lila to move away from the tree. Away from Leo.

She got it. Still holding her cheek, she inched away from the tree toward Justin hedging in the bushes.

Leo spun around. "What are we going to do now?"

Lila stopped about halfway between him and Leo, both brandishing guns.

Leo's dark eyes narrowed. His gun dangled at his side. "You're not much good to me now, are you?"

Throwing her hands out, Lila said, "I've given you all I know. Let me go. Let my son go. You can retire to your island retreat, and Justin will never find you."

Leo snapped, "I can't do that. This was to be my last assignment for Al Tariq. A lot of money is riding on this."

She stepped farther away from Leo. "Surely you have enough money to be comfortable now."

Leo sneered. "There's never enough money."

He stalked toward her and jerked her arm, pulling her toward him. Nudging his gun against her head, he asked, "What are you to Lone Wolf? More than just a convenient bed partner? Does he care enough for you to tell me where that damn tunnel is? Because I'll bet my own life he knows."

Justin couldn't have asked for a better opportunity. He stepped into the clearing, gun cocked and raised. "Let her go, Leo, and I'll tell you where the tunnel is."

Leo crowed. "Lone Wolf himself. I knew I could count on you."

Leo pressed the barrel of his gun to Lila's temple. Rage seared through Justin's blood, bringing it to the boiling point. He felt his eyes brim with the heat.

"Let her go, Caine. You still have her son. Let her go, and I'll take you to the site myself."

Leo pulled Lila closer. "Do I still have the son? Maybe, maybe not, but you never cared much for kids anyway. No, I'll keep the lovely Lila and you'll take me to the tunnel."

Justin said, "Just call your people, and I'll tell them where it's located. Then you can release her."

Leo laughed. "Nice try, Vidal. So I release her and my associates go out to find nothing at all, or worse, a trap? Then I'm dead."

Justin shot back, "Then take me."

Lila cried out, "No."

Leo twisted her arm behind her. Justin shortened the distance between them, but Leo dragged Lila back.

Leo replied, "No thank you. I think I'll keep what I

have. You seem to want it so badly. I'm surprised at you, Lone Wolf."

Justin burned with frustration. He'd never realized what a sadistic streak Leo had. But then, how well did he really know the man? After those first few years of training, he'd pushed Leo away every time he tried to get close, fearing the connection he felt with him. He regretted it now.

Leo continued, "I'll tell you how it's going to be. Lila and I will follow you as you lead the way to the tunnel. That way, if you play any tricks or set a trap for me, Lila dies."

A muscle twitched in Justin's jaw. If Leo saw the Border Patrol, Molina or anyone else at the tunnel location, he'd kill Lila—even if he couldn't get away himself. He'd kill Lila. He had to call off the ambush.

He clenched his jaw even tighter. If he called off the ambush, Leo would get away. He'd notify his Al Tariq contacts and he'd get them and their materials through the tunnel before the HIA or Border Patrol could stop them.

Leo confirmed his supposition. "Before we reach this elusive tunnel, I'll call in the Al Tariq operatives who are standing by just waiting for direction. As long as all goes smoothly, I'll give Lila back to you."

He chuckled, "Of course, Al Tariq's men and supplies will already be through the tunnel by that time, and I'll be on my way to paradise—and I don't mean the kind with fifty virgins waiting for me. Although I think I can arrange to buy a few virgins where I'm going."

Justin growled, "Straight to hell."

Leo answered, "Perhaps. In the meantime, what a

dilemma for you. Of course, if all Lila means to you is a good lay, your choice is simple."

Lila's eyes, huge and glassy, sent a torrent of anger surging through Justin's body.

She choked out, "Tyler."

Justin felt Lila's fear smother him like a blanket of dust. He couldn't bear it. He had to offer her some relief, some pinpoint of light on which to focus.

"Tyler's okay. I found him in the warehouse. He's safe."

Leo sucked in his breath and swore.

Lila sank to her knees, Leo's gun tracking her head. She whispered, "Oh God, thank you."

She raised her blue eyes, shimmering with hope, to Justin's. "Thank you for saving my son. I knew… I'm sorry—"

He cut her off harshly, "Forget it." He didn't want her apologies for leaving him.

The news of Tyler's safety began to act like an elixir on her. She brushed her hands across her face, now beginning to swell on one side. As she rose from her knees, her back straightened, and she shoved Leo's gun away from her head.

Her eyes narrowed, piercing Leo with their blue light. "Do what you have to do. Justin's not taking you or your Al Tariq murderers to the tunnel. If he does know where it is, it's probably destroyed already."

Leo's pebble eyes grew round. His grip on his gun faltered.

She laughed, a harsh, grating sound that cut across the still clearing. "I was just a good lay."

Justin shouted, "Stop it, Lila. I'm taking him to the tunnel."

She jerked her head toward him. "As long as Tyler's safe, that's all that matters. If he shoots me, shoot him back. That'll end it. No tunnel. No terrorists. No attack."

No life. Justin's face felt carved from marble. He had to bend to Leo's wishes. Had to take him to the tunnel. Had to keep Lila safe for as long as possible.

He cranked his head from side to side. "No."

He extracted his cell phone from his pocket and called Molina. "It's Vidal. Call it off. Change of plans."

Facing Caine, he said, "The tunnel's in Quietas Arenas, close to the Mexican border where California and Arizona meet."

Lila brought her hands to her mouth, her eyes wide above them.

The corners of Leo's mouth turned up in a semblance of a smile. "You had it all worked out, didn't you? Such a good plan, too. Lead me and my Al Tariq associates to the tunnel and have a little party waiting for us. But you figured correctly. If I see any hint of an ambush, sweet Lila dies. Who would've guessed Lone Wolf could be brought down by love?"

Justin looked at Lila still in Caine's clutches. Despite her anger and fear, she radiated. Her sun-kissed skin glowed and her deep blue eyes shined with an inner light. Love?

He felt it now—that tightness in his belly had been slowly unfurling ever since he looked into those blue eyes. Now it reached out to every cell in his body, nourishing it, nurturing it. Even now, in his darkest hour, he felt invincible.

Their eyes locked. She felt it. Sensed it. Sensed his power and its source.

He turned and strode toward his truck. "Follow me."

Leo's fingers pinched into her upper arm, and he kept his gun trained on her as they followed Justin's purposeful figure out of the clearing.

She floated along beside Leo, the pain in her arm where he gripped her and the throbbing of her cheek both muffled by the patina of joy that encased her. Tyler was safe. Justin saved him.

How many times had she wronged the man in her heart? And still he came. She didn't doubt him now. Couldn't doubt the love that glowed in his amber eyes, enfolding her in a sweet caress. She took strength from it.

Leo shoved her into the driver's seat of the car. He grunted, "You're driving."

By force of habit, she snapped on her seat belt and adjusted the mirrors.

They followed Justin's truck, serving up dust and gravel from the access road, as he wheeled onto the strip of asphalt. She drew closer to his bumper, and Leo barked, "Slow down. Not so close."

Lila shot him a sideways glance. What was he afraid of? Afraid Justin would slam on his brakes? She looked beyond him out the window. The asphalt broke away to a soft shoulder comprising more gravel and even more dirt.

Leo kept his weapon pointed at her with one hand while he fumbled for his phone with the other. He removed his seat belt to get the phone out of his pocket. He put it on speaker and carried on a short conversation in Arabic before ending the call.

Lila bit the good side of her lip. He'd already made his plans. Once they got to the tunnel, Leo's cohorts would be there to meet them. They'd slip into the country with their deadly materials, assemble their weapons of terror and carry out their attack.

Stealing another look at *el diablo*'s profile, she knew he'd never let her live. He'd never let Justin live. He hated Justin with the fierce hate only envy can spawn. Justin embodied everything he wanted to be.

Couldn't Justin see that? With all his years of experience, couldn't he understand they were just buying time? And the price was their country's security. He was risking it all. Risking it all…for her.

The road swam before her as her vision blurred. The well-worn sign for Loma Vista floated before her.

Where it all began.

She jammed her foot on the accelerator. The back of Justin's truck rushed at them. Leo cursed and leveled his gun at her head with an unsteady hand. With her left hand, she jerked the steering wheel to the right, throwing Leo against the passenger door. She swept her right arm up and out, catching Leo's forearm. The bullet exploded through the roof of the car.

Justin's brake lights loomed ahead as Leo lowered his arm for another shot. Lila yanked the wheel again to the right, stomping on the gas pedal. The car crunched through the gravel and dirt as the tires attempted to grip the road. They gave up.

The car lurched forward, striking a rise on the shoulder. Leo squeezed the trigger again as his head flew back against the window. The bullet and the window cracked at the same time.

Lila felt a hot blast in front of her face and released the steering wheel. The car jumped, airborne, until it careened onto its side. Lila's body snapped in space. Dust and glass hurled through the air. She squeezed her eyes shut against their assault.

One low thud and then silence except for a spinning, whirring sound. Lila peeled her eyes open and stared through the windshield, cracked into hundreds of stars. Her body felt suspended and she couldn't turn her head with the seat belt digging into her neck.

She heard a voice above her. Justin's voice.

"Oh my God. Lila, are you all right?"

She groaned. Her face throbbed, her chest hurt and she couldn't move, but other than that…

His voice, low and steady, touched her ear. "Listen, babe, reach down with your right hand and release your seat belt. Don't worry about falling. I've got you." The door squealed as he opened it, sending a blast of hot air into the car.

Moving her fingers down her side, she felt for the seat-belt strap and followed it down to the buckle. It took all her strength to press the small release button. When it clicked, her body dipped sideways, but Justin had his arm wrapped around her.

The smell of gasoline flooded her nose, and she kicked her legs instinctively to scramble from the car.

He whispered, "Shh. It's okay. I'll get you out before…"

She choked. Before what? Before the car exploded? The smell of gasoline permeated the air…and something else. The acrid smell of smoke.

Justin's strong arms pulled her up from her tilted

seat, her legs dragging over the upended doorjamb. Once she was free from the car, he scooped her up and ran across the road.

The explosion ripped the air behind them, pieces of metal and glass resounding in a cacophonous racket.

His large frame covered hers, and she sank under his weight. With the fire now crackling in the background, he looked into her face, raising one eyebrow. "I have a bad habit of winding up on top of you."

Through her pain, she managed a wicked smile. "Next time we'll have to change positions."

He didn't move, instead pulling her tighter into his arms. She didn't have enough breath to tell him he was squeezing her sore ribs. Then when he started landing kisses all over her face, she didn't have the heart to tell him he was hurting her sore cheek. She gave herself over to the pain…and the pleasure.

She placed her hands against his chest, his shirt now soaked with sweat. "Caine?"

Rising, he pulled her to her feet and gently turned her toward the flaming car tipped on its side, its front wheel still spinning. "Even before the explosion, the jolt threw him from the car. He's crushed between the side of the car and that embankment."

Leaning against him, she folded his arms around her. He hugged her, and she winced.

"You're bleeding."

She looked down at her ripped sleeve. "I think it's from the glass."

He swept her up in his arms and carried her to his truck. "You took a huge and stupid risk."

She burrowed her head into his shoulder and said,

"Haven't you realized that I do stupid and impulsive things all the time."

"That stupid risk saved the day, and you didn't even use an incantation, did you?"

Her eyes watering, she shook her head. Their love had been strong enough.

He settled her on the seat of the truck, kissing her hard on the corner of her mouth.

As he turned the truck around, she asked, "Where are we going now?"

"You need to get bandaged up." He flashed her a grin. "And there's someone in Loma Vista I think you want to see."

They drove up to the same dusty café where she'd discovered Chad's letter directing her to see Justin Vidal. The same place where she'd discovered a dead body in the trunk of Chad's car. She shaded her eyes against the sun and saw three figures standing on the porch. Two men…and a boy.

She jumped out of the truck before it stopped and ran to Tyler, catching him in a hug. Her tears dampened the top of his head. For once he didn't squirm in her grasp.

Later, after they called the Federales to report the accident and after Leo's body was recovered and taken away, they all sat at one of the little scarred tables in the café before plates of food. Lila tilted her head at Justin. "How did you know where the tunnel was? Or was that a ploy?"

He grabbed her hand and raised it to his lips. "No ploy. Look."

He smoothed the map in the center of the table and

pulled a piece of paper from his pocket. Laying the paper next to the map, he said, "Look at the name of this town."

She read aloud the name circled in pencil, "Quietas Arenas. So?"

"So, Chad was shot before he could finish his sentence. He wasn't yelling *'El túnel está aquí.'* He was trying to say, *'El túnel está a Quietas Arenas.'* Quiet Sands, the name of the border town near Arizona. The real location of the tunnel."

Tyler's eyes shined. "Sweet. It was like a puzzle, and you figured it out."

Lila sat forward. "Shouldn't we be headed up there right now? Caine made a phone call before I ran the car off the road. I'm sure he was giving whoever was on the other end directions to Quietas Arenas."

Justin pushed a plate of food toward her. "Let's hope so. While the proprietor's wife was bandaging your many wounds, we took care of that. The Border Patrol, HIA and CIA are already on it. They'll probably converge on Quietas Arenas about the same time as Al Tariq. They'll stop them."

She studied the three men at the table. "Don't you want to be there? You figured this out. You followed it through."

The three exchanged looks and smirked. Molina said, "Glory? We don't need no stinkin' glory."

Justin explained, "We like to keep a low profile if we can. We don't want anyone from Al Tariq to identify us, so we can just slip into our next assignment."

Lila's heart skittered in her chest as she stabbed a piece of chicken on her plate. His next assignment?

Epilogue

The weeks following their showdown with Leo Caine in Mexico passed without incident. No mention on the news of any tunnel in Quietas Arenas. Other than the Padres losing the first game of the World Series, the event took place without a hitch.

The two weeks she spent on the run could've been a dream. Almost.

Lila sighed and clicked the print button. The last pages of her report on the fluorescent strawberry anemone of La Bufadora hummed through the printer. No research trips this quarter. She'd be in the classroom lecturing for two quarters before her next jaunt.

She pushed back from the computer, slumping in front of it. When she got back from Mexico, she'd been ready for another fight. A fight with Gareth over Tyler. But the fight never materialized. Gareth called her, strangely subdued, to tell her he and Liz were taking an extended business trip to Europe. He didn't mention any lawsuit, didn't castigate her for Tyler's kidnapping.

Tyler had been clingy and nervous after Mexico, but

once he started school and got back into the rhythm of his ten-year-old life, he seemed to settle down.

He didn't talk about his kidnapping or what happened in Mexico except to ask about Justin. Seems he'd made a pretty strong impression on Tyler.

Made a pretty strong impression on her, too.

She gulped down a sob, which rose up through her nose anyway and burned her eyes. He'd seen her and Tyler to a hospital in San Diego, made sure they were both okay and taken off…on his next assignment.

She bounded up from her chair and grabbed a tissue from the bathroom. Okay. The sex was great, but she couldn't expect anything more from a man like that. Even though…

He'd put everything on the line for her. That was more than lust. She blew her nose. Didn't matter. She had a class to prepare.

As she crouched before her bookcase, the phone rang. Even if it was Tyler calling her from his cell phone for about the tenth time today, she'd forgive him. She'd been so happy to have him back and safe, she let him keep the cell phone.

"Hello?"

"Lila, it's Justin."

Butterflies fluttered in her belly as she clutched the edge of the bookcase.

"Lila?"

Feeling light-headed, she sank to the floor, crossing her legs beneath her. "Code name?"

He drew in a breath and chuckled. "Lone Wolf 58634, but I'm changing that. In the meantime, you need to report immediately to my safe house."

All her nerve endings tingled at the sound of his sexy voice, and his light, joking manner filled her heart with hope. She'd report to Mars to see him again. "Will I be safe at your safe house?"

"You know the risks."

She knew them and was willing to take them. Even for one last time.

JUSTIN STRAIGHTENED the carved maple dining-room table in the little kitchen and positioned the four matching chairs with their blue fleur-de-lis–embroidered cushions around it.

Flowers. He needed flowers in the middle of the table.

He glanced outside to the tangled garden in front of the house. He needed a gardener.

After arranging a bunch of scraggly flowers in a vase, he placed it on the table. He frowned. Were those flowers or weeds?

Lila's voice lilting over the phone eased his soul. She sounded happy. Was she happy to hear from him or was she happy there were no more threats from her ex-husband? Justin had seen to that.

Seems Stone owned a manufacturing plant for computer parts. Justin made it clear to Stone that he'd send Immigration on a raid to the plant if he didn't halt his plans to challenge Lila for Tyler's custody. Stone dropped the custody idea pretty quickly and decided he needed to make a business trip out of the country. Of course, Justin's threat of bodily harm helped Stone's decision.

Pacing the floor, he glanced down at his watch. His cell phone rang, and he checked the display before groaning and stowing it in his shirt pocket. Kate again.

Seems the meeting with their father was a success. Kate assured Justin he'd changed, stopped drinking and wanted to beg their forgiveness. Now Kate planned a big family reunion, and it looked as if he might be headed to Hawaii on his next vacation. Kate couldn't wait, but the thought of seeing his father again made his mouth go dry.

A few months ago, he would've refused to go, but now he knew he had the capacity to forgive, to trust, to look ahead instead of being dragged down by the past.

He shoved his hands in his pockets and waited by the window. The unmistakable growl of a Porsche's engine echoed down the street. The sleek black car slid up to the curb, and his sleek golden girl slid out of it.

He opened the front door as she skipped up the walkway. Extending his hands, he pulled her inside, saying, "I need to ask your advice about something."

Those beautiful lips, all the swelling gone now, curved into a smile. The beautiful eyes followed with an upward tilt.

Propelling her to the dining-room table, he asked, "What do you think of this?"

Knitting her brows, she ran her hands over the smooth polished surface of the table. "It's a beautiful piece."

She touched the petal of a yellow flower hanging over the edge of the vase.

"Do you like them? Uh…those were kind of last minute."

Her velvety lashes swept down over her eyes. "They're lovely."

Weeds. She still sucked at lying.

Leading her into the living room, he said, "There's

one more thing I want to show you." He tipped the back of a cane rocking chair, sending it to and fro.

She sank into the chair and looked just as he'd pictured her in it. "Now, this is lovely." She stopped rocking. "Why are you showing me this furniture? Is that why you called me?"

He looked down at her, longing to sink his fingers into the curls that danced on her shoulders. "I just want to make sure you like it."

A rose flush crept into her cheeks. "Why?"

He knelt down next to the rocking chair. "Because I want you to move in here. I want to furnish this place like it should be. Like a home. Do you think that second bedroom is big enough for Tyler?"

She traced her finger along his jawline and whispered, "What about your next assignment?"

He grabbed her hand, chaffing it between his two palms. "I already have my next assignment."

Withdrawing her hand, she looked away. "You once told me your job and marriage didn't mix, family didn't fit it."

"That's right."

She jumped up. "Tyler and I can't live like that. I'm fresh out of magic rituals, Justin, and I'm not going to try to turn you into a salesman. I can't sit and wonder every day whether or not you're in danger."

Wiping a hand across her eyes, she said, "Even though that's exactly what I've been doing ever since you left us in Mexico."

He cupped her face in his hands. "Have you?"

She leaned in for his embrace, and he wrapped his arms around her, resting his chin on top of her head.

She said into his chest, "I mean it, Justin. I love you, but I can't…"

His hold tightened. "I love you, too, and I can't, either."

Drawing back from him, she looked into his face. "What are you saying?"

He laughed. "Don't worry. I'm not going into sales. My next assignment for the HIA is to oversee training. Although how I convinced them I should be in charge of a bunch of green recruits is beyond me."

She drew in her breath and dived back into his arms. "You'll be wonderful."

He pulled her into the bedroom. "I plan to be wonderful…right now."

He started unbuttoning her blouse as he kicked off his shoes.

Snatching at his roaming hands, she laughed. "What are you doing?"

His words nuzzled into her neck as he pulled his jeans open and dropped them. "We're going to christen another piece of furniture."

Following his lead, she wiggled out of her skirt. "This bed is not new, and we've been here before. Twice."

He dragged her panties down over her silky thighs. "That's right, and the last time we were here, you sneaked off after you had your way with me."

She giggled as his tongue trailed over the swell of her breast. "As I recall, you had your way with me. I was sore for days after."

"Serves you right." He fell onto the bed, pulling her on top of him. "Different position, remember?"

Her mouth was too busy for a reply, so he crossed his hands behind his head. His cell phone rang, and he slipped it out of the pocket of his shirt now hanging open on his chest. Lila never raised her head.

Kate. More news about their father and his family, no doubt. He peeled his shirt off and tossed it onto the floor. His cell phone followed.

Time enough for that family. He wanted to concentrate on the one he had right here at home. His home.

* * * * *

Turn the page for a sneak preview
of the first book in the new miniseries
DIAMONDS DOWN UNDER
from Silhouette Desire®,
VOWS & A VENGEFUL GROOM
by Bronwyn Jameson

Available January 2008
(SD #1843)

Silhouette Desire®
Always Powerful, Passionate and Provocative

Kimberley Blackstone didn't notice the waiting horde of media until it was too late. Flashbulbs exploded around her like a New Year's light show. She skidded to a halt, so abruptly her trailing suitcase all but overtook her.

This had to be a case of mistaken identity. Surely. Kimberley hadn't been on the paparazzi hit list for close to a decade, not since she'd estranged herself from her billionaire father and his headline-hungry diamond business.

But no, it was *her* name they called. *Her* face was the focus of a swarm of lenses that circled her like avid hornets. Her heart started to pound with fear-fueled adrenaline.

What did they want?

What was going on?

With a rising sense of bewilderment she scanned the crowd for a clue, and her gaze fastened on a tall, leonine figure forcing his way to the front. A tall, familiar figure. Her head came up in stunned recognition, and their gazes collided across the sea of heads before the cameras erupted with another barrage of flashes, this time right in her exposed face.

Blinded by the flashbulbs—and by the shock of that momentary eye-meet—Kimberley didn't realize his intent until he'd forged his way to her side, possibly by the sheer strength of his personality. She felt his arm wrap around her shoulder, pulling her into the protective shelter of his body, allowing her no time to object. No chance to lift her hands to ward him off.

In the space of a hastily drawn breath, she found herself plastered knee-to-nose against six-feet-two inches of hard-bodied male.

Ric Perrini.

Her lover for ten torrid weeks, her husband for ten tumultuous days.

Her ex for ten tranquil years.

After all this time, he should not have felt so familiar but, oh dear, he did. She knew the scent of that body and its lean, muscular strength. She knew its heat and its slick power and every response it could draw from hers.

She also recognized the ease with which he'd taken control of the moment and the decisiveness of his deep voice when it rumbled close to her ear. "I have a car waiting outside. Is this your only luggage?"

Kimberley nodded. "I assume you will tell me," she said tightly, "what this welcome party is all about."

"Not while the welcome party is within earshot. No."

Barking a request for the cameramen to stand aside, Perrini took her hand and pulled her into step with his ground-eating stride. Kimberley let him, because he was right, damn his arrogant, Italian-suited hide. Despite the speed with which he whisked her across the airport terminal, she could almost feel the hot breath of the pursuing media on her back.

This was neither the time nor the place for explanations. Inside his car, however, she would get answers.

Now that the initial shock had been blown away— by the haste of their retreat, by the heat of her gathering indignation, by the rush of adrenaline fired by Perrini's presence and the looming verbal battle—her brain was starting to tick over. This had to be her father's doing. And if it was a Howard Blackstone publicity ploy, then it had to be about Blackstone Diamonds, the company that ruled his life.

The knowledge made her chest tighten with a familiar ache of disillusionment.

She'd known her father would be flying in from Sydney for today's opening of the newest in his chain of exclusive, high-end jewelry boutiques. The opulent shopfront sat adjacent to the rival business where Kimberley worked. No coincidence, she thought bitterly, just as it was no coincidence that Ric Perrini was here in Auckland ushering her to his car.

Perrini was Howard Blackstone's right-hand man, second in command at Blackstone Diamonds, a legacy of his short-lived marriage to the boss's daughter. No doubt her father had sent him to fetch her; the question was *why?*

* * * * *

*Get swept away down under with the glitz
and glamour of the Blackstone empire
as Kimberley tries to determine the real reason
behind her "reunion" with Ric....*

*Look for VOWS & A VENGEFUL GROOM
by Bronwyn Jameson,
in stores January 2008.*

Silhouette® Desire

When Kimberley Blackstone's father is
presumed dead, Kimberley is required to take
over the helm of Blackstone Diamonds. She
has to work closely with her ex, Ric Perrini, to
battle not only the press, but also the fierce
attraction still sizzling between them. Does Ric
feel the same...or is it the power her share of
Blackstone Diamonds will provide him as he
battles for boardroom supremacy.

Look for

VOWS &
A VENGEFUL GROOM

by

BRONWYN
JAMESON

Available January wherever you buy books

Executive Sue Ellen Carson was ordered by her boss to undergo three weeks of wilderness training run by retired USAF officer Joe Goodwin. She was there to evaluate the program for federal funding approval. But trading in power suits for combat fatigues was hard enough—fighting off her feelings for Joe was almost impossible....

Look for

RISKY BUSINESS

by

MERLINE LOVELACE

Available January wherever you buy books

REQUEST YOUR FREE BOOKS.

2 FREE NOVELS PLUS 2 FREE GIFTS!

◆ HARLEQUIN®
INTRIGUE®

Breathtaking Romantic Suspense

YES! Please send me 2 FREE Harlequin Intrigue® novels and my 2 FREE gifts. After receiving them, if I don't wish to receive any more books, I can return the shipping statement marked "cancel." If I don't cancel, I will receive 6 brand-new novels every month and be billed just $4.24 per book in the U.S., or $4.99 per book in Canada, plus 25¢ shipping and handling per book and applicable taxes, if any*. That's a savings of close to 15% off the cover price! I understand that accepting the 2 free books and gifts places me under no obligation to buy anything. I can always return a shipment and cancel at any time. Even if I never buy another book from Harlequin, the two free books and gifts are mine to keep forever.

182 HDN EEZ7   382 HDN EEZK

Name	(PLEASE PRINT)	
Address		Apt. #
City	State/Prov.	Zip/Postal Code

Signature (if under 18, a parent or guardian must sign)

Mail to the Harlequin Reader Service®:
IN U.S.A.: P.O. Box 1867, Buffalo, NY 14240-1867
IN CANADA: P.O. Box 609, Fort Erie, Ontario L2A 5X3

Not valid to current Harlequin Intrigue subscribers.

Want to try two free books from another line?
Call 1-800-873-8635 or visit www.morefreebooks.com.

* Terms and prices subject to change without notice. NY residents add applicable sales tax. Canadian residents will be charged applicable provincial taxes and GST. This offer is limited to one order per household. All orders subject to approval. Credit or debit balances in a customer's account(s) may be offset by any other outstanding balance owed by or to the customer. Please allow 4 to 6 weeks for delivery.

Your Privacy: Harlequin is committed to protecting your privacy. Our Privacy Policy is available online at www.eHarlequin.com or upon request from the Reader Service. From time to time we make our lists of customers available to reputable firms who may have a product or service of interest to you. If you would prefer we not share your name and address, please check here. ☐

H

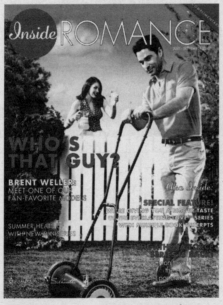

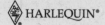

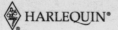